To Michell

thank you for supporting me. I do hope you enjoy my stories & looking into my strange mind. You are such an inspiration to me, so for you to read my work is <u>thrilling</u>! Good luck on your own journey!

Hummingbird Tales

stories and creative nonfiction by Brittney Kristina

Keep flying!

Brittney

Copyright @ 2021 by Brittney Kristina.
All rights reserved. This book or any portion thereof may not be reproduced or used in any manner whatsoever without the express written permission of the publisher except for the use of brief quotations in a book review.

Printed in the United States of America

First Printing, 2021.

ISBN: 9798469707554

Independently Published with Kindle Direct Publishing

Cover Design by Jared Atkins.

There are always too many individuals to thank, so really, thank *you*, for reading this work.

But, on a serious note, there are some people I'd like to recognize.

To Jared, the one who understands me most. Thank you for being my number one supporter and best friend.

To my parents, who have helped guide me, so far, through this bewildering yet beautiful life of mine.

To James, a fellow sensitive artist. This book, quite literally, would have never been published without you.

"Don't bend; don't water it down; don't try to make it logical; don't edit your soul according to the fashion. Rather, follow your most intense obsessions mercilessly."

- Franz Kafka

Table of Contents

8 | Introduction

Part One: Backwards, Straight Down
15 | How to write a book in 4 easy steps
19 | Sleepwalking
23 | Always Slightly Past
25 | The Confrontation
29 | The Dragon's Curse
33 | Hypocrites
35 | The Disappearing Man
40 | The Dead Night
44 | Never-Ending Express
49 | Part of The Family
54 | Memories of It
60 | Vortex
65 | Crimson Tie
75 | Sister of Sleep
79 | No More Real Than Water
81 | The White Room

Part Two: Simply, At Rest
89 | Coyote
100| I Am Here
103 | Swimming
107 | What A Lovely Day It Is
110 | Ghosts of the Sea
112 | A Strange Observation
117 | I Don't Remember Much

121 | You're Not Real
131 | Something Outside My Window
135 | It Wasn't Me
139 | She Was There, And Then She Wasn't
147 | She Looked at Me
149 | Versions of Myself
158 | Alone, Together
163 | Is This Life Not Already Enough?

Part Three: Forwards, Straight Up
167 | This Is What Strength Looks Like
170 | Scars
173 | Mending her Own Tears
177 | I Know A Place
180 | I Will Remember You
186 | Mother and I
189 | Going on A Walk
198 | The Night I Saw Him One Last Time
202 | The Girl with The Book
204 | The Most Interesting Man I've Ever Met
209 | Too Good for Me
211 | Loose Threads
217 | Devoid of Expression
231 | Transformation
239 | The Colors of Me, of You, of Us
245 | The Tale of the Hummingbird

250 | Afterword
252 | Welcome to the Mind of a College Freshman

Introduction

Why, hello there.

So, you may be wondering why I've titled this collection of stories and creative nonfiction "Hummingbird Tales". You also may be wondering why I, a novelist, decided to publish a collection rather than another book. Surprisingly, both wonders are interconnected. Let me explain.

Although it's been three years since I've published a novel, I've been writing. While I've dabbled in other novels, I've mostly worked on short pieces. This is primarily because when I'd sit down to write my next, "better" book, I'd crumble, have difficulty finding my footing even when I had done it twice before. Or, the idea of writing another book was simply too daunting for me at that time. So instead, I'd write stories. Personal pieces. I explored all types of genres and tropes and relaxed while I did it, had fun while I did it, the stories pouring out of me naturally and temporarily taking away the pressure to write another novel. One day, I realized I had written 45 stories and creative nonfiction pieces, and an idea sprung. *This* idea. At first, and for a while, really, I'd talk myself out of publishing these pieces. The familiar voices, the imposter syndrome, the comparison crept up from the shadows and haunted me, kept me stuck. Perhaps fellow creators can understand this feeling.

The pieces in this collection remained untouched, gathering dust in my documents. The pieces weren't good enough, weren't polished enough, were too vulnerable, too real. Too me. *Right?* Furthermore, who was *I* to publish short stories? But, when I thought back to my younger self, who fearlessly published *Forsaken*, then *Fifty Days*, not caring what anyone else thought of her, just wanting to create, express herself, show the world what she could do, who she was truly, inside… well, I felt inspired by her. The young me, who had a dream, stood up against the familiar foe, imposter syndrome, and did it.

    And so, this is me doing it. Fighting back against the what-if's, the doubts, and believing in myself and in my creations. I mean, what's the worst that could possibly happen?

    I have only shown parts of myself, online, to others. No one has truly stepped into my head, and no one truly will, of course. But oftentimes I notice myself hiding, sheltering behind a smile, a joke, a pretty feed, my truth manifested into a fictional character so that I can step back, safe, and feel comforted in the fact that no one can see inside, can see the *real* me, sheltered behind this brick wall I've built around myself.

    But these pieces, all of them, are probably the most "me" I can possibly get. Some are fictional, some not, some carefully crafted and heavily edited, some written quickly, remaining raw as they were first written. Some have clear plot, clear purpose, others meant to be interpreted, contemplated on. These pieces are glimpses into myself, into my mind and what I fear most, and what I ponder on when the world around me is quiet. I explore heartbreak, death, life, grief, love, and everything in between. Fantastical worlds, introspective trains of thoughts, relationships held together by falsities, strange yet beautiful people. And all this time, I have been chasing these ideas alongside myself, cracking open my soul and pouring out everything I have ever felt or imagined onto the pages. I've learned so much about myself with the assistance of these pieces.

Of course, my novels are parts of me as well. In fact, both *Forsaken* and *Fifty Days* helped me tremendously during difficult times in my life, those times having projected onto the characters, onto the plot, the books tearing off huge chunks of my soul and therefore representing my growth, and who I used to be. I was able to explore my hardships through the lens of someone else, in another world, in a vastly different situation, and in theory, *heal* myself through writing.

However, there's something different about the pieces in this collection, I think. Of course, you can read them for yourself and perhaps you'll agree, or perhaps not. It is fine either way. These stories are yours now, to dissect and take as your own, anyway. Yet, unlike my novels, in these stories, I am raw, I am real, I am unapologetically me, and I don't hold anything back.

Oh, how terrifying the thought is, that you are journeying into my mind, taking me as I am, looking at me up-close and personal. But, how exciting it is! You are here, in my mind, with me now. I hope that these pieces make you feel less alone in whatever you are going through or have gone through. I hope that you see me, as I see me, and in turn, see yourself. Yes, these pieces are mine, but they are also yours. I do hope you enjoy them, the scattered and lopsided and unique shards of myself.

I realize I have never answered the Hummingbird question.

Elizabeth Gilbert, author of *Eat Pray Love*, gave a speech called Don't Chase Your Passion And Maybe You'll Find It in which she distinguished the difference between Hummingbirds and Jackhammers. Jackhammers, according to Gilbert, are people who have one goal, one interest, one passion, and work diligently to the end. Hummingbirds, however, have many interests, flutter from one desire to another, constantly changing their dreams, goals, trying to squeeze themselves into boxes rather than exploring everything they like or have interest in. They live life how they think they *should* rather than how they truly want to.

I, a Hummingbird, took this message to heart, realizing that all my life, I had been trying to squeeze myself into the "right" version of me, living as though I were a Jackhammer. I was writing pieces others expected me to write, acting as a young girl in her 20's should, living life how anyone else would, with one goal, one path, working diligently toward one ideal life.

I would sit down with myself and write these strange, dark, introspective stories and quickly, I'd hide them, because they weren't stories people predicted I'd ever write. And they were so… *different,* I had doubted anyone was have true interest in reading them.

As you can imagine, this limited me from creating what I truly wanted to, from living my life in a way I felt called to. I felt trapped, stuck. This is another reason why I had talked myself out of publishing these pieces for so long—they are so up-close and personal, so unlike what is expected of me. It wasn't until I emerged from the box I built for myself, and allowed myself and my passions to roam free, that I was able to embark on the scattered, beautiful path paved out for me.

I am a person of many interests. I adore all genres, love trying out new writing styles, tropes, and different perspectives. I flutter from idea to idea, chasing my passions and obsessions maddingly, never once limiting myself. These stories and creative nonfiction pieces reflect this, I believe, all so different yet all still *mine*.

My stories, as mentioned above, explore several topics, and not one is like the other. Therefore, when staring at my colorful array of pieces, trying to pry out a title to summarize them all, I fell short. That is, until I remembered Gilbert's speech, and the name naturally flourished into fruition.

Hummingbirds have rather unique bones and muscles in their wings, allowing them to fly backwards, straight down, forwards, and straight up. They can also fly in place; simply, at rest. These pieces, although all equally parts of me, have been divided--there are times when I feel as though I am flying backwards, straight down, and there are times in which I am gliding, forwards, straight up. There are other times when I am simply, at rest. Therefore, the stories are laid out as such. Scattered, moving in different directions, bouncing from one to another, just like the hummingbird. Just like me.

Admittedly, I've been going on in this introduction for ages, so I presume you are ready to dive in now, to see what these strange, dark, introspective stories are all about.

I am a hummingbird, and these are my tales.

Part 1

Backwards, Straight Down

How to write a book in 4 easy steps

Hi there!

As you may, or may not know, I am an author of two, psychological thriller novels. Because many aspiring writers have requested to know how I did it not just once, but *twice*, I've decided to write a blog post explaining my entire novel-writing process in just 4 easy steps. Enjoy!

---

1. Return to your past to seek out your idea

I'll let you in on a little secret: my book ideas stem back into my childhood, whether I'm consciously aware of it or not. With a blend of suppressed trauma, heartache, fears, and fluctuating mental states that I am currently enduring, my story idea emerges. I suggest addressing any unresolved issues of your past and extracting the story's brilliant purpose from the ashy ruins locked away deep within your mind. But, then again, the idea will continue to change and expand over the course of your novel, so don't stress about it too much. The story doesn't have to be fully fleshed out. At least, not yet.

Now that you have your (loose) idea, what's next?

2. Crack open your shell and look at yourself straight-on

Now that you've uprooted your past, it's time to face yourself straight-on. Doing this will help you in creating authentic characters with real issues. I recommend staring at yourself in the mirror while you cry. However, I can understand why this may feel uncomfortable. Normally, I instead achieve this by unintentionally crafting my main character to be like me in every sense applicable. They then undergo a series of psychological ventures that are really just metaphors for those uprooted, un-processed wounds of mine. Therefore, I can chip away at the shell I've encased myself in and catch a peak of not only my main character and the direction they're headed in, but at my inner turmoil as well!

3. Bleed

Okay, okay. It sounds difficult, but it's honestly not so bad. Simply claw the skin of your face and carefully peel it off, all the way, as though it's a latex suit, and hang it up in the bathroom so that you can pull it on again later. At this point, you will be bleeding a large amount, and that's okay--this is supposed to happen. Eventually, the blood will begin to carry your fingers across the keyboard, and the muscles and tendons on your bare hands will dance and your laptop will be strewn with red, and your bedroom will be strewn with red and *you*, my dear, will be red all over and entirely naked to the world and the story before you and you'll bleed like you never thought you could bleed before. It may be painful, but it will be wonderful! Trust me.

In no time, your story will pretty much write itself, with the help of your blood, of course. And when you're done for the day, you can stretch your skin back over your body. Be sure to use bleach for the carpet! And don't worry about the bruising.

4. Polish the blood

Unfortunately, no one wants a blood-soaked book to read. So, when your book is complete, and after you've edited it a few times through, be sure to polish the excess blood you've shed so that it doesn't *look* like blood, but it *reads* as though whatever blood remains was intentional, as though the blood belongs to the *character* and not yourself. This way your readers, your friends, your family… they won't worry about you. Because you don't want them to. You're fine, really. No, *really*, you are. It's just that, without pain, you cannot seem to create art. At least, not the same kind of art, with that same sort of depth. The people who know you will tell you that they couldn't put the book down, that they were completely immersed, that the main character was oh-so relatable, that your story was "deep" and "moving", and you'll smile and thank them, and it'll feel good, and in time, when you're ready, you can begin a new novel. This time, with new wounds to dig up, a new shell to crack through. A new self to look at straight-on.

See? Writing a book is not so bad.

Thank you so much for reading my post! Also, sorry it's a day late--unfortunately, I had a big exam the day before and didn't have time to write it.

I really hope my 4 tips have helped you in writing your book, but feel free to message me if you have any questions or would like some more insight.

Have a lovely rest of your day!

Probably writing,
Brittney

Sleepwalking

I awake to the feeling of grass beneath my cheek, moist and scratchy on my skin. My dewy eyes open slowly, the lids heavy, and I blink until my surroundings come to fruition. The moon, bright and bold above my head, encases me in a brilliant, milky illuminance. Surrounding me are towering oak trees, their leaves swaying against the hum of the light breeze, cool and dry on my skin as it grazes past. I assume I am dreaming, and my eyes slip closed, my body curling into a comfortable fetal position. But, when the feel of the grass beneath me doesn't dissipate, and a harsh wind blows between the trees, creating a sharp whistle that bounces off the night air and nearly pushes me over with its force, my eyes jolt back open. I scan my surroundings, which look so vivid, feel so real, the smell of dampened greenery and fresh air overwhelming my senses, and that's when it hits me: I'm not dreaming. No, not at all.

Hurriedly, I rise. I'm wearing my gray pajama pants, a black tank top, and I'm barefoot. Quickly, I recall that this is the very outfit I wore to bed the night before. *I think.* So, sometime between 11 pm last night and now, I winded up in a forest. *How?* No, the answers don't matter right now. What matters now is getting home.

Tense with both confusion and uneasiness, my gaze twists around, looking for a direction to head toward. But everywhere I look, I am faced with the same sight: trees, their outlines brought forth by the moonlight, followed by more trees. Between the trees, there is only blackness. A *hoot* erupts from within the forest, and I jump in a panic, my neck twisting to search for it. But I am faced with only darkness. *God, I'm so skittish*, I think to myself. *Just start walking, and you'll be home soon, surely.*

Mere moments later, a violent, gut-wrenching scream erupts from the exact direction I started walking in, and then another, raspy and cracked along the edges. Overwhelmed by fear, my heart pounding maddeningly in my chest, I pause for a moment, hesitating as though unsure whether this is real, or a falsity. Then, just as a third scream screeches, closer this time, my legs give out beneath me like limp noodles, carrying me far into the opposite direction. Unsure of where I'm going, where I'm headed, I race deep into the night. My breathing is fast and loud, as I am not a runner, or in any great physical health at all, really. My throat constricts, my calves already knotted, two rocks aching. Raspy screams ricochet from all directions, far away but close enough, seemingly coming from deep within the forest and following me, right on my heels like emancipated dogs. The screams, they echo, hanging in the damp air like a thick fog that fills my lungs and settles there. I try not to pay attention to them, focus only on running, faster and faster still, my breath white in the air, my chest tightening with exhaustion, my legs stiffening, my right foot tensing with a cramp. I land on something hard and sharp as I run, and my teeth grind together in response, a moan escaping from between their grit, yet I continue onward, feeling the wound swell as I do.

Suddenly, a scream bellows right in front of me, so close I can feel the hot, thick breath on my face. I jolt backwards, panting heavily as I search into the trees, but there is nothing but that familiar, dense darkness. Endless, never-ending darkness. The screams, they go off all at once, nearing slowly, closing in on where I stand. My palms press against my ears as I slip down to the earth, my knees hitting the soft, cold grass beneath me. I close my eyes and wait. I have nowhere to go, nowhere to hide. I'm so incredibly far from home. So, lost.

Then, just as the screams are warm on my face, stroking my skin like gentle hands, yet painfully sharp in my ears, they hush, vanishing mid-scream, and everything is quiet. "Beth?" my father's voice calls from beyond the silence that surrounds me now.

My eyes peel open and are blinded by bright daylight. Squinting, I glance around to see the familiar oak trees, their leaves glinting sunlight. Songbirds flutter from branch to branch. It is peaceful, almost too peaceful. The sun is warm on my skin, blanketing me with comfort, and safety. My dad, along with a few police officers and people I recognize as neighbors are approaching me, relieved smiles plastered on their faces, yet their foreheads wrinkled with concern.

"Dad?" I ask, still blinking against the brilliant, yellow light all around.

"Beth," he says as he approaches. Then, he drops onto the grass and holds me tight. "Oh, Beth. Where were you? Why are you in the woods? You're three *miles* from home, and we were worried *sick*--"

"I… I don't know, Dad," I say, exhaling deeply into his embrace. Around us, people are whispering to one another, their voices drenched in worry, the police officers muttering into their devices, which crackle. "I… well, I woke up here."

He chuckles, shakes his head, and I notice his left eye twitch, just slightly. "Oh, Beth, you were probably just sleepwalking."

My left eyebrow lifts. "I do that?"

"Oh, well everyone does. Eventually."

I sigh, lower my gaze. My skin continues to tremble, memories of the screams racing through my mind still, all that I can hear, the darkness all that I can see. "Dad… I'm still so scared. I… I had such a terrible dream."

"Oh, Beth, it's okay. It's not a dream anymore. Now, you are safe, at last. Where you belong. With me."

I grin at this, nodding. My eyes lift and it is dark now, and my dad, who is not quite my dad, sits before me, an uncomfortably wide grin stretched onto his face. The police officers and neighbors, who aren't quite police officers nor neighbors, sway in the breeze like balloons, or empty sacks, frowning.

"We will keep you safe," my dad continues. "You will be safe here. With us. We are all so happy here, aren't we?" He turns to face the weightless people behind him.

At that, they part their lips, and they scream.

Always Slightly Past

I see a woman off in the distance, staring at me with beading eyes. It's the same woman. It always is. She has a small frame and sharp cheekbones, wearing only a light pink nightgown, which fits her a little too big. Her face is narrowed down as she glowers in my direction. If I look closely, she's not even staring at me but at something slightly behind me with a crazed look in her eye, as though there is something dangerous just beyond my right shoulder. When I turn my head, I see her, standing near, but not too near, just enough so that I can smell her breath, feel her warmth wafting off her like a summer breeze. She's staring at me, but not at me, her blue eyes shifted slightly away from me so that she's not looking at me, but at the second version of herself, directly ahead of us. And when I look ahead of us, she stands there, staring at the second version of herself, but this time there are more, *several*, all standing there, looking just beyond me. I shift my head over my shoulder to see her once again, but now there are more, they have expanded, and there are too many to count, more versions of herself than stars in the entirety of the universe. Beneath me, there she is, and above me, there she is. Everywhere I look, there are more. I am trapped within this ever-expanding paradox of versions of this woman, staring at herself, but then again, never quite at herself, always slightly beyond. The more I follow the eyes, the more clones I am greeted with. She blinks, once, and at the same time, they all blink, perfectly synchronized. Besides her, there is only a cold, bitter darkness that fills the space between them. This goes on for a while, me looking back and forth and all around, and each time, the quantity of her grows, the empty space so thick with black that I feel trapped and deprived of air. I find myself gasping for a full breath, closing my eyes so that the women disappear, only to find that they're still there, under my eyelids. Every breath is icy-cold in my throat and contains little air. I clutch my neck and collapse to the floor--but I find that there is no floor, only emptiness, only *her*, so I continue to fall, grasping at my chest, trying to breathe but finding that the darkness, the eyes, begin closing in. I am nothing and I am everything.

After a while of endless falling, my eyes lift just slightly, and at last, meet hers. I'm not sure what to make of it at first, but I look into her, and she looks into me, and for a brief glimpse of time, we are connected, we are one, and through her tears that have just begun to form, she smiles. We smile. All of them, they smile, perfectly synchronized.

This is when I wake up, every time. Every morning. And every morning, I crawl out of bed, and walk to my floor-length mirror, and look at myself. At the girl with the small frame and sharp cheekbones and blue eyes, at the too-big, light pink nightgown. And, as much as I want to, I never look her in the eyes. I can't, I just can't. Not yet. I just stare, slightly to the right, never directly, until the dream has mostly diminished, and I go on with my day.

The Confrontation

Pacing, pacing, pacing. How long have I been here, just pacing? I'm alone, or at least seemingly alone for now, on a wooden bridge above a gentle stream in the middle of the night, in the middle of the darkness. Pacing, pacing, pacing. My fingers alternate inside my mouth as I gnaw on one, then another, my cuticles bleeding and my nails shortened to almost nothing. Occasionally, I chew on the inside of my mouth, and that too bleeds from the slits where my teeth lay pressing. I even scratch at my wrist, worsening the rash that appears each winter due to the harshness of the cold air. My breath is white. My feet are numb. My heartbeat flutters rapidly at the base of my throat. And I'm pacing, and pacing, and pacing.

It's not the fact that I'm alone, a mile deep inside the woods behind my house, nor the fact that it's dark and all I can see is the ripple of the stream, the pale leaves, all brought forth by the bold moonlight. It's what's to come. It's the moment he arrives, which could be any moment now.

I'm not ready. I'm not sure why I decided to do this. Or I suppose I know *why*, but I never wanted to come here. I was trying to avoid it for as long as possible, really. But I suppose I couldn't handle it any longer; the sound of leaves crunching beneath his hunting boots as he wanders, all throughout the night; catching him in windows, peering at me from behind the trees. I *must* make it stop. And this is the only way, as far as I can tell. At least, it is the only thing I haven't tried yet, confronting him, confronting *it*.

I stop pacing, grip the railing of the bridge, and peer over at the flowing water. It ripples and glistens, racing across rocks and forming along the curvatures of the stream. The water hums, trickling as it passes, a lovely, fluid song against the night sky. I breathe in deep, filling my lungs with dry, sharp air, and exhale, watching my smoky breath dance in the air. *Relax. Calm down. It'll be over soon. You'll be okay.* But the words mean nothing to me. They do very little. I gnaw at my fingernails again and taste the metal of my blood.

Pacing, pacing, pacing. I continue pacing, but not for much longer. I blink and I'm sitting, unsure of how I got there, so incredibly dizzy. My head bows forward, and I close my eyes, the sound of the steam and the thump of my heartbeat all I can hear, besides the occasional rustle of the leaves. It's peaceful here. It really is. I could stay here for a long time. Maybe fall asleep.

If only he weren't coming. If only he didn't dominate these woods now. Because when he finds me, I'll have to admit it. I'll have to face it. I'll have to face what I have done.

I breathe in, breathe out, each breath becoming thinner, harder. My body shivers against the cold, or maybe the worry? I can't tell at this point. I just keep breathing. Scratching. Biting. Shivering.

The sound of footsteps in the distance, leaves crunching beneath hunting boots, causes my head to spring up, my eyes now wide and frantic, searching. The internal chaos that once was dominating me has fled and has been replaced with stillness. I'm a deer in headlights. Frozen in place.

A silhouetted figure saunters behind the trees. *Can he see me? What the hell am I going to do when he does? What am I going to say? Why did I come here?* I know why. I needed it to stop. It *needs* to stop. I cannot take it any longer. This must be the only way.

I wait.

And wait, and wait, and wait. Watching him appear, then vanish once again behind the trees. Eventually the footsteps near, and soon enough, he's here, standing on the bridge, staring down at me. He wears dark clothing and a look of despair, or confusion. His expression sinks in but shows no sign of vengeance. His skin, I notice, is pale, nearly transparent, and his eyes are dark, and my stomach twinges at the sight of them. He used to have tan skin, bright eyes, a warm smile. I remember loving him. And now he stands here, almost limp, a shell of who he used to be, and the love is gone. I try not to lower my eyes to his chest, but I can't help it. They drift down to the bullet wound, the tear in his shirt just above it. His chest is pale, like his face, the wound purple. It happened so long ago.

My eyes lift back up to his as I stand, slowly, trembling at either the sight of him, or the cold? Once again, it's hard to tell.

"I-I'm sorry," I tell him. "I really am. I'm so terribly sorry." His face remains the same, unmoving.

"Can you please… finally forgive me?" And my bottom lip trembles as I add, softly, "*Please.*"

The Dragon's Curse

Her eyes are clouded—controlled. She is one of them now.

How typical of them, to turn the one I loved most into this ruthless, powerful being. She looks at me, clutching her knife tighter. Her face is straight, unmoving. Human features carved into stone.

"Ella?" I whisper, extending my hand toward her, looking deep into her bright, white eyes, which only moments ago were bold and brown and *hers.*

She swipes her knife at me, and I jolt back, my teeth clenched as the aching pain that comes with loss, the *tears,* press their way through. But I must force them back. And I do.

They laugh around me, and I look at them, scowling at their white eyes and scaly, long, *dark* faces. They are mostly hidden by shadows, and yet, I can still see them. How I was so fooled by them, I have yet to know. I suppose I was desperate. We all are in these regions.

I turn back to Ella. Black scales bubble up along her arms like boils, and she simply stands there, allowing it, transforming into the abominable *things* that these creatures are. So badly, I wish to reach out to her, feel her one last time. But it is too late.

They drew us here, urged us to come inside and trade. How foolish of me to think anything else of them -- they only wanted *us*. They never want to *trade. How terribly foolish of me!* They wanted to expand their army; I should've known. All Ella and I wanted was supplies, as we are only starving travelers, bonded lovers. Or *were*. Who knows what our fate entails now.

The leader, I presume, lifts a claw, his scales brought forth by the glittering light from the cracks in the ceiling above. In a hoarse voice, he says, "Now, it is *your* turn to join us." His claw remains extended, purple magic swimming about the air around him, and crashing down at me in waves. The purple light presses me back, and so I lean forward to strengthen my stance. The magic floods into me, absorbed by my skin, and I feel it within me, swelling. I am surrounded by this purple light, breathing in the overwhelming fumes, and I can feel my entire body expanding, pulsating against this curse.

The darkness melds into me, sinks into my skin, and I wait. My eyes dart to Ella's stone face as I say to her, knowing she can longer hear me, "I'm so sorry." I feel myself carefully turning into this hideous beast that Ella, once a beautiful and young elf as I, has now become. I watch her grow, now unrecognizable, her snout extending and her fangs elongating. And I wait.

And nothing happens. I glance down to my hands, but they are still mine, and I am still conscious. Still here.

They don't seem to notice this. But Ella does. *Ella!* I stare deeply into her eyes, and faintly, I see her, crying out to me, her soul pressing itself against the scales, trying to escape this new body of hers. And yet, is too late. I know it, and so does she. She will be trapped here, alongside these beasts, and I cannot save her. I do not have the magic to combat such a curse.

An idea springs. A terribly sad idea, but an idea to prevent Ella from being entirely trapped.

And so, I charge at her, as a distraction, and this dragon beast who has overtaken her swipes at me again with her knife. I pretend as though she has harmed me, fling myself down to the ground and hit the stone, hard, moaning out into the open air and grasping my bicep, all the while still staring into Ella's eyes. Although the beast rages, the Ella within calms, and she understands what I am doing.

Slyly, I create some magic of my own, putting to practice one of the only spells I remember Father teaching me. I roll onto my side, away from the beasts who watch me from the balcony, proud as I seemingly struggle, so I can formulate my trick. And I continue to moan, wail, growl, pretending as though I'm changing. But I must hurry, because certainly it is obvious that I have remained the same.

I look at Ella and smile. I can see her inside, still, if I squint enough. She is calm, accepting. "I'm so sorry, my love," I say again, so softly only she can hear. "But it is what must be done. I will see you soon once I too am laid to rest."

With a mighty blow, I release a wave of searing flames from my palms, surprised at the force of it and at the fact that I even executed it correctly, and the beast that once was Ella roars and collapses to the floor, eaten alive by the fire before my very eyes. The flames consume the palace, climbing up pillars and rising toward the leader, who roars maddingly as the fires blanket his scales.

Frantically, they search for an escape. But they are trapped. The creatures screech out as the balcony of the palace cracks and rumbles, plummeting toward the earth, bringing the beasts down with it.

I stand and dash away quickly, darting toward the entrance of the palace and pushing open the two, hefty doors, the flames nipping at my heels, rocks falling and barely missing me. For once, I am lucky. I run through the tunnel Ella and I were led down into only moments ago, and I emerge quickly, being greeted by the mighty trees and greenery of the forest that Ella and I had been traveling through for many months. It is still early in the day, the sun rising over the valleys, the birds awakening from slumber with songs. It is so peaceful, despite the roar of the fallen palace behind me. How familiar it all is, the peaceful forest. How terribly sad it makes me.

I glance back, watch as the glimmering, golden structure is consumed as though a feast, eaten alive by the flames. A few tears fall--I allow it, as this is a proper time for them to appear.

"Goodbye, for now, my love," I mutter, taking one final glance at the fire before turning away and running deep into the forest forevermore.

Hypocrites

I drink an energy drink from an aluminum can and toss it into the plastic Kroger bag lining the inside of the plastic trash can beneath my plastic desk while I watch a YouTube video titled "how you're funding climate change and you don't even know". The video opens up to the 2015 Paris Climate Accord in which almost every major country came together to prevent climate change. This agreement's goal is to keep the global temperature increase of this century beneath two degrees celsius. I notice that everyone at the conference is wearing plastic name tags standing in front of paper banners and the audience is recording everything on their iPhones.

Since 2015, JP Chase Morgan Bank has invested more than $269 billion in fossil fuels, and I scoff. I think, *how dare they?* Later that day, I drive to Target, fill up my gas tank along the way, buy a new pair of inexpensive workout shorts, and I swipe my Chase debit card and take my paper receipt and drive back to my apartment.

More than one trillion plastic bags are used each year, and 100 million barrels of oil are used to manufacture that much plastic. Apparently, there are over 15 trillion pieces of plastic waste in our oceans. My boyfriend rants to me about climate change, my roommate panics at the thought of rising temperatures, and I start to hate plastic, too, and try to buy items packaged in glass when I can. (Each year, 10 million metric tons of glass are thrown away, and only one-third of all glass gets recycled.)

Sometime that week, we all go grocery shopping together and we bag our groceries in those thin, plastic bags because I accidentally left my plastic but *reusable* bags in the car and I don't feel like walking back out to fetch them. (Did you know that you can reuse plastic grocery store bags?)

On my walk to class, I notice all the trash dotted along the streets, tucked against curbsides, floating in little streams, and I feel sad about it, but I don't stop to pick anything up because trash has germs and I'm already late.

Later that day, I watch a bird peck at a cigarette butt and swallow it whole and fly away and motionless, I watch it and think to myself, "What a silly bird." I continue eating my sandwich composed of organic lunch meat and produce and then I dump my trash into a trash can outside of the classroom.

The next morning, I buy some sustainable products from Amazon and feel good about myself, especially after hearing about their 2019 climate pledge. The products come in a cardboard box with plastic lining and so I remind myself to recycle it all, forgetting that my apartment complex does not recycle. I feel bad, compiling so much trash. But, as my friend says, "An individual alone cannot stop climate change."

Sometimes, I do pick up trash. I whisper to trees, stroke their trunks with my fingertips, feed squirrels pieces of my uneaten granola bars, toss french fries at birds, and as I do these things, simple, almost meaningless tasks, I think to myself, "Look at me, I'm changing the world."

The Disappearing Man

I first noticed my reflection seemed off a few months ago, when I glanced at a mirror to see only a haze where I stood. When I blinked, rubbed my eyes with my fists, my reflection returned to normal and without much more thought, I carried on, blaming the illusion on my lack of proper sleep.

Two days later, the familiar haze stood in place of myself in the bathroom mirror above my sink. The haze, although wearing my clothes, was only a soft, white glow, dark splotches in the places my eyes normally resided in. Within a few moments, my normal self materialized, and all was well again, mostly. I brewed myself an entire pot of coffee, because surely, I was heavily sleep-deprived, then returned to my research per usual.

One might consider me a quiet man. The only person I regularly stayed in contact with was my mother, whom I had a falling out with and hadn't spoken to in several months at that point. She was quite mentally ill, which led us to unfortunately experience some disagreements. In fact, the more I pondered on it, I hadn't interacted with anyone in quite some time, as I hadn't exactly left my home. But this wasn't something I minded or even something that made me sad. I rather enjoyed being alone, and always had. Growing up, I never had many friends, nor acquaintances, and spent most of my days reading novels and later, textbooks on Neuroscience. To cure cancer with only the mind, this had been my research goal since I was 19. And at this point, when I had begun seeing things in the mirror, I was 46 and almost complete with my article, my world-changing research. Without much social interaction, I had plenty of time to work on what mattered most to me, so in the end, the thick silence that filled my apartment, when I wasn't otherwise playing Beethoven softly, was a gift, rather than anything *sad*. No, my quiet life wasn't sad at all. Although, I did greatly miss my mother. She was the only person who truly understood me.

      A few days after my second bewildering reflection experience, another occurred. But this time, blinking and rubbing my eyes didn't help. In fact, I remained only a haze, two dark smudges on a white glow with a slight outline of a nose. I never saw my true self again, as it only worsened from there; eventually my peppered hair also became just a haze, as did my clothes, and soon enough, the glow that was myself in the mirror became entirely translucent. I would spend hours staring at my reflection, unsure of what to do and reluctant to call anyone about it, as it was so utterly bizarre. I considered seeking psychiatric help, but my stubbornness prevented me from proceeding. 27 years of studying Neuroscience and I hadn't the slightest idea of why I was seeing myself as a sheer illuminance against my apartment. It wasn't only the mirrors in my home, either; it was all of them. I'd go on a stroll solely to pass mirrors in stores or stop above a puddle on the sidewalk, just to see if I was visible. However, I'd peer down only to be faced with the same image, that white glow now tinted blue against the sky above. I also began to observe how no one seemed to acknowledge me, or if they did, it took them quite some time to notice me standing there. They'd laugh at themselves, call themselves blind, but it was never the slightest bit humorous to me.

"So, you *can* see me?" I'd ask them.

"Of course," they'd say.

That was at least minorly reassuring.

Yet overtime, my reflection continued to dissipate, becoming more and more transparent until I could make out only the slightest outline of where my clothes and hair sat. Before long, there was no one looking back at me from the mirror. Terrified, I went out on another stroll so that someone would acknowledge me and I could prove to myself that I still existed. Yet, no one did. That was the first day I realized that not only was I invisible to myself, but I was now fully invisible to everyone around me. If I talked loud enough, their ears would perk up, and their eyes would scan the area where I stood, but never once did they stop. When I drifted past them, they'd shudder, as though cold. But never once did they see me.

I began to wonder if I had died. If I had, yet somehow had no recollection of it. I couldn't help but wonder if I was only a ghost, but not yet aware of it. It was a ridiculous idea, however, and I had a good laugh with myself after thinking of such an insane thought, but the laugh left my presence quickly and I was left with only anxiety, only fear. At that point, I had no clue what was happening to me, and I couldn't continue lying to myself. I was truly horrified.

One day, a man walked right through me. That same day, I decided to call my mother for the first time in nine months.

"Hello?" she said after answering on the third ring. Her voice had worn like yellowed paper, and the sound of it flooded me with warmth and wholeness for the first time since I first saw the haze in the mirror where I stood.

"Mother, it's me. Richard. I'm so glad to hear your voice," I said. "Something strange has happened to me."

"Hello?" she asked again.

"Mother, can you hear me?"

"Richard, is that you? Oh, Richard. Please. Is that you?"

"Yes, Mother, it's me!"

"Richard… oh, how I miss you dearly."

"Mother! You can hear me!"

"Oh, I hope… I hope he calls me soon."

"Mother? I'm here! Can you… can you hear me?"

The line went dead, and I sank into the floor, then I sank through the floor. Where I went, I'm not entirely certain. But it is like I disappeared, forever, sinking deeper and deeper, vanishing without a trace. Only my nearly-complete research left, where someone might stumble across it, one day, in time.

No one ever saw me again. But then again, had anyone truly seen me before? I was no longer alive, or at least no longer present in the world, but when I truly thought of it, I don't remember having been present ever, in my entire life. Therefore, I suppose, disappearing didn't impact me as much as I originally predicted--I rather enjoy the quiet. It's so quiet now, way down here.

The Dead Night

The sky darkened, stars protruding from the edges of the horizon, the moon strikingly full above my head. I was an idiot, having forgotten that out in the woods, service wasn't really a thing, and yet I decided to rely on Google Maps rather than a physical one. In my defense, it was my first time hiking alone, and the trail was only a few miles from campus--it wasn't like I was descending deep into the vast, Rocky Mountain National Park. I knew where I was. Well, in regard to the city, the general area. But, in relation to the forest, I had no earthly idea. And I was tired--I don't remember having walked so far before then. I was still new to hiking, to exercise, even, and at that point it became bluntly obvious. My quads quaked and my calves pinched as I strode uphill, in the opposite direction that I first walked in, back toward campus--I think--and my lungs swelled with damp, warm air, my breath harsh as it puffed out into the summer night. Fireflies emerged from beyond the trees, lighting trails for me against the darkening path, and gnats flew swiftly around me, resting on my sweaty skin, and my shirt clung to me uncomfortably. I felt miserable. Whoever insisted that hiking was fun? Why would wandering alone in the woods with burning legs and nothing to do but to listen to the sounds of nature, be *fun*?

I halted, dropped my backpack from my shoulders and shuffled around inside for my water bottle, retrieving it and sipping down the last few ounces I had saved. The water was cold, refreshing, and I savored it on my dry tongue, letting my mouth bathe in its chill. And then, it was gone. With one granola bar left--an *idiot*--I was certain I was screwed.

My eyes trailed the forest as I tried to assess where I was. I couldn't have walked *too* far into the forest, dammit--it was a nature trail after all, and I had been walking since noon. I had heard no people for the entirety of the day, nor did I even hear cars trailing by on the distant gravel roads. Had I simply gone down the wrong trail without realizing? I knew I must have because certainly, I should have been back home by then, lounging on the couch, binging Doctor Who and vowing to never step foot in nature again. Quite possibly assuring myself I'd never exercise again.

That's when I saw it, the haze of a flame illuminating on far-off trees. The sound of crackling fire was carried toward me along with the scent of something savory and sweet, like roasted, spiced meat. Without hesitation, I slung my backpack over my shoulders and sped-walked toward the fire, the bottoms of my feet curling in my sneakers at the formation of tightening cramps, even my *abs* feeling sore and overworked. God, I was still so thirsty, my mouth filled with sand, and hungry, my stomach roaring with churning, a deep pit of tightening emptiness.

I approached to see a man who wore a black jacket, the hood shadowing his face and leather gloves stretched over his thin, bony hands, hovering over a fire, a freshly caught squirrel rotating over the rising flames. Not familiar with someone eating squirrels, I took a few steps back, my stomach plummeting at the sight. In doing so, the man heard me, lifted his still-shadowed face to stare at me. And yet, I could not see his eyes.

"Hello," he said in a voice that sounded rusted, as though it hadn't been used in years. It had little emotion to it, completely monotone, yet not unfriendly. "Care to join?"

"I, uh…" I trailed off, still eyeing the squirrel, it's flesh charring and cracking into a leathery texture. Its eyes had been melted off, leaving two empty sockets. I shuddered. "I was just wondering if you knew where we were. I'm… I'm a bit lost." Nervously, I chuckled, still maintaining my distance.

The hooded man stared at me through the darkness. The sky had gone black then, revealing millions of bright stars. I had never seen stars so bright, so close, in all the years that I had lived in this small town, even against the light of the fire.

Finally, he spoke, "You are in The Dead Woods."

"The what?"

"The Dead Woods," he repeated. "It is at the edge of the civilian walking trail."

"Oh," I said. "Well, do you know how I might get back to the, uh, civilian walking trail?"

He stared at me again. Then, he laughed. Like his voice, it sounded rusted, as though it had chipped away over time, sprinkling dust over the ground as he used it. "If I knew how, I wouldn't be here."

I blinked. "E-excuse me?"

"You don't remember," he said, "but you will, overtime. We all do, eventually." He lifted his gloved hands, his fingers prying off his hood and revealing a mostly skeletal face, only a few pieces of skin and bare flesh barely hanging onto his left cheek bone, along with a singular, brown eye loosely rotating within the socket. My chest lurched, and I gagged at the sight, and then I was running, madly into the night, far from the campfire.

At least, as far as I could manage to run; my legs gave out beneath me, and I fell, plummeting down the side of a hill, tumbling like a rock. When I landed, I laid there and breathed, heavily. *It wasn't real. It's not real*, I told myself, my mind racing and my entire body stiff with fear.

In time, my eyes peeled open. Before me rested a small puddle of water tucked into a crevice of the earth, and I crawled toward it, carefully, slowly, quietly, in case he heard, in case he *was* real. When I was near enough, I dipped my face down to stare at my reflection. And that's when I noticed my throat, which had been slit open, the blood now darkened, dried on my skin.

Never-Ending Express

    I board the train in nothing but my boxers, brown mountain boots without socks, and a red robe, my bare skin dry against the harsh, cold air. There's a snowstorm tonight, which is strange--there are rarely snowstorms like this in my hometown. But then again, there's rarely any trains, either, especially not ones that arrive at your house during the middle of the night. *But*, I remind myself, *it is only a dream.*

    The conductor, his dark eyes shaded by his blue conductor hat, smiles sloppily at me, revealing yellowed, decaying teeth as I step inside. I don't remember why I decided to climb onboard. Perhaps because I often feel brave in dreams. I shudder, either from the cold or the sudden heaviness that penetrates from the train. Tugging the robe over my mostly naked body, I round the corner to find several adults and a few teenagers and children seated in luxurious, red-leather seats pressed up against frosted, gold-rimmed windows. They're all facing forward, and although my boots certainly cause the metal stairs to squeak under their weight, creating an echo effect throughout the train, nobody turns to look at me. No one is speaking to each other, just staring straight forward as though lost in a daze or entranced by an imaginary movie playing just beyond their eyes. Stiffly, I walk forward into the train, looking at the fellow passengers as I walk past. Their eyes, shrunken and dark, like the conductor's, stare lifelessly ahead, their mouths small and lips pressed together softly. It's difficult to tell whether they are even alive. This thought frightens me and in turn, my head fills with a sudden pounding and an eagerness to get off and go back home. My head whips around and I start to turn back, but by then, it is too late. The door has shut, and the conductor is standing still against it, his hands clasped in front of him, his chin dipped down. However, I'm most certain I never heard the door slide closed. Perhaps I was too distracted by the unnerving sight of the passengers to hear it.

The train's horn bellows into the night and, soon after, churns into motion. My body sways forward at the sudden movement and I nearly topple over but catch myself just in time by clasping a nearby seat and pressing my boots into the floor. The woman sitting on the seat I lean on angles her head toward me, slowly, her face as still and lifeless as stone. Her pale skin sags and her brown hair has begun graying, her eyes boring into mine. Carefully, a smile etches onto her face. "Are you excited?" she asks me, her voice cheerful but in a peculiar way, like it is not her own. Almost as though the voice belonged to her years ago and hasn't aged alongside her appearance.

"Excited for what?" I ask her. My voice trembles, and I pity myself for it. *It's just a dream*, I remind myself. *It has to be.*

"Why, excited to ride the train!" she exclaims, revealing chipped, blackened teeth. Her breath, even from where I stand above her, smells like rot. I wince away from her. "It is just the most thrilling experience."

"Where is it taking us?" I say, stepping away from her, feeling unsettled by her unblinking eyes.

"Why, to the North Pole, of course!"

"What for?"

The woman laughs hoarsely into the air, but never replies to my question. When she is done laughing, her head twists back around to face forward, almost automatic, and certainly unnatural, and her smile slips off, revealing no trace of any previous laughter.

My body slides into a nearby seat toward the front, as far from the other passengers as I can manage, my shoulder pressed against the window, which is bitterly cold to the point that it burns. But I don't withdraw my shoulder. My eyes stare aimlessly into the snowstorm, hoping to see something to distract myself from this terror I'm currently in. But I am only faced with a never-ending darkness and the occasional wisp of snow against my window. Any sign of my neighborhood or the nearby city is nowhere to be found, as though we are already miles away from home.

A while later, the train rolls to a stop and the conductor steps out into the storm. I hear some chattering, a slight confusion and evident hesitation from a second voice outside. Then, it is quiet for too long. After what feels like an entirety of sitting, waiting, wondering who else could be boarding, soft footsteps pad down the hallway between the seats. I glance over my shoulder to see a young woman about my age, early twenties, her arms crossed over her chest and her face wrinkled in horror and uncertainty. She slides into the seat just behind me, her eyes searching the stoned faces around us. The train, just as before, screams into the night before jolting forward then speeding up toward our unknown, ambiguous destination.

"Hey," I say.

Her eyes dart to meet mine, filled with panic. Quickly, she turns away, avoiding my gaze.

My brows furrow in confusion, yet I go on: "Are you okay?"

The woman glances toward me, her body leaned back, and her chin angled down, as though trying to hide somehow. Her green eyes are dewy and her pupils are wider now. "Where are we going?"

"Why, to the North Pole, of course!" I tell her, a soft smile spreading onto my face.

At the sight of my smile, she trembles away. With a small, shaky voice, she asks me, "What for?"

My smile fades, and I shake my head. "Not sure. I suppose we'll find out?"

The woman turns from me and stares out the window, although her eyes are unfocused, looking at something in her mind rather than beyond herself. "It is just a dream," I hear her tell herself. Her expression, overtime, hardens, and her eyes darken and sink down into their sockets. She never speaks to me again.

Eventually, I readjust myself forward, feeling the train hum beneath me as it travels across the tracks, my body swaying side-to-side with its rocky movements. My eyes trail toward the window to face an everlasting night once again. For some reason, I feel as though it's been night for an awfully long time. I feel like, at this point, I should've woken up from this nightmare.

A reflection appears in the window, or perhaps I just hadn't noticed it before, and my eyes lift to meet it. Staring back at me is an old man, his skin wrinkled and folded, deep bags under his eyes. His red robe is tattered with holes and streaked with something crusty and blackened. I smile at the reflection and notice his rotten, mostly decayed teeth when he smiles back at me. I can smell his stench even from the other side of the window. Matter of fact, this entire train is stale with a thick scent of withering, like aging leather, which I haven't noticed until now. The woman behind me, who has fallen especially still and has become frail and bony, smells the worst of them all, her stench mixed with the slightest hint of citrus and vanilla. An old perfume, I assume.

Although the train rolls to a stop every now and again, welcoming on more confused passengers, the train never returns me home, nor do we ever arrive at the North Pole. In fact, the train keeps moving, indefinitely, and time becomes nothing more than a thought. It feels like just moments ago I had stepped onto this train, and yet, I've been here for so long that I can no longer remember my name.

Part of The Family

MaryAnne Jones brought a boy over. Her and the boy, Josh, had been dating for a couple of months, and so MaryAnne insisted he stop by to say hello, introduce himself. It's time you meet my family, MaryAnne told him. They'll love you. Of course, Josh had his doubts, was afraid they wouldn't like him, since he was shorter than most of the other boys at school, but he knew he loved MaryAnne, and he knew it was time. So, he agreed.

They stepped into the Jones' little, blue house, which sat at the corner of Oak Street, just two blocks from the high school, and Josh caught a whiff of the strangest smell. Mrs. Jones perched straight up and stared at Josh from the loveseat she resided in each day. Josh smiled boldly, MaryAnne glanced away, shielding her eyes, and Mrs. Jones remained unmoving. She pressed her lips together and her eyes seemingly grew larger on her face. Josh stirred, a bit uncomfortable now, then said, Hello. After a few moments, which to Josh seemed to have lasted an eternity, Mrs. Jones laughed. It was a loud, ear-splitting laugh that rattled the vases and trembled the floor beneath Josh's feet. Mrs. Jones wore a smile ear-to-ear while she laughed, unnaturally large and deep, revealing a full set of pearly white teeth. Guests! She exclaimed. I love guests!

Her lips pressed back together as she stood from her chair, rather rigid, as though she hadn't risen from her chair in quite some time. In fact, she hadn't. Mrs. Jones had not left her chair in eight days, not even to use the restroom. Josh could smell her from where she stood. A strong odor of urine and sweat filled the air with a thickness. Josh held his breath. MaryAnne was used to it.

Mrs. Jones wore a bright, hot pink dress that cinched at the waist and fell around her knees, and she wore hot pink pumps to match. Her clothing fit her stiffly but faltered her well. Her dress seemed newly pressed, besides the urine strains. Her platinum blonde hair was curled and framed her face perfectly. Her face, too, was beautifully structured, with high cheekbones and brilliant blue eyes. Her pink lips remained pressed together in a too-wide smile. She did not resemble MaryAnne in the slightest. MaryAnne was also perfectly structured, with a symmetric face and bold, brown eyes with naturally curly black hair that carried not even the slightest bit of frizz. However, MaryAnne had a wider nose, a thinner neck, a curvier build. Josh wondered if MaryAnne better resembled her father. But MaryAnne did not. Her father rounded the corner the moment Josh had this fleeting thought, and he stared Josh down with a stern gaze. Mr. Jones had red hair that stuck straight up and a thick yet perfectly combed red beard and rounded green eyes with a bold, broad figure. Mrs. Jones, Mr. Jones, and MaryAnne all had different eyes, different bodies, different faces, as though they weren't at all related. But Josh knew genetics could be strange sometimes. And who knew--perhaps MaryAnne was adopted, and she simply hadn't mentioned it before.

Guests, Mr. Jones said, glancing between MaryAnne and Josh. He said *guests*, as in a plural form, just like Mrs. Jones. Then, just like Mrs. Jones, he laughed. His laugh, however, was sharp and sliced the air with a depth that only someone as bulky as Mr. Jones could produce. He was truly a terrifying man.

Come in, please, Mrs. Jones said. However, Josh wasn't certain he saw her lips move because her smile remained, just as abnormally wide on her face. The smile shook Josh to the core. He turned his head to look at MaryAnne, but her face had sunken, her eyes small, her lips small, and she stood as still as stone. Josh wasn't sure if she was even breathing. MaryAnne, he said. Her eyes lifted and she grinned, but that was all. In fact, MaryAnne was terrified for Josh. She knew what her parents would do to him, exactly as they had done to everyone else, including her, and all she could think about was how foolish she was to bring him here, and how she should've brought someone else, someone less likeable, with less of a future. However, she didn't exactly have a choice. She never really did.

Come in! Mrs. Jones bellowed, her voice once again shaking the vases. It is time for dinner. But she didn't move, only stood there, smiling widely and unmoving. Mr. Jones's stern face returned. Like MaryAnne, they stood there, so still, not even breathing, he was certain of it, just staring. Josh inhaled deeply, then continued into the house. At this, Mrs. Jones hastily turned into the kitchen, her heels clicking against the hardwood, a bit too suddenly, Josh noticed. The house seemed normal, decorated with vases, colorful rugs, blue and white pillows with cream throw blankets, and picture frames of... nothing. Josh blinked at the frames, which were empty, but *not* empty. There were deep holes within the frames, revealing a darkness that sunk into the house. When he turned his head, the entire family, including MaryAnne, was seated at the kitchen table, beaming at him, and fresh, savory food covered any empty space on the table, hot and steaming and ready for Josh. Any recollection of the picture frames fled his mind; he had completely forgotten what he had seen yet remained unnerved.

How did you two meet? Mrs. Jones asked Josh and MaryAnne once Josh had slipped into his seat. He parted his lips to speak, and then the strangest thing happened; he forgot. How long had they been together? When did they meet? All of this information seemed to slip his mind, and so MaryAnne answered for him, We met in Science class, Momma. We were lab partners. It hit him then; oh yes, lab partners. How had he forgotten? The memory of her sliding next to him, immediately drawing his interest, appeared bright and bold in his mind. In fact, he even remembered passing her a note, asking her to be his girlfriend, and out loud, she told him yes.

How had he *forgotten*?

How sweet, Mrs. Jones said. Her lips still hadn't moved.

Josh glanced down at his plate to see it overflowing with turkey thighs, mashed potatoes and gravy, roasted carrots, two buttered biscuits, corn, and applesauce. He wasn't hungry, but didn't want to come across as rude, so he proceeded to eat. While he ate, he didn't notice that Mrs. Jones and Mr. Jones and MaryAnne were staring at him, smiles vanished from their lips, and none of them ate their food. Because they didn't need to eat anymore. They watched him, blank-faced, as it happened.

Swiftly, as though time had become elastic, it was night. When he finished his food in silence, his eyes lifted and he noticed children standing in the window to the backyard, all with dark eyes, hands pressed to the glass, watching him, but when he blinked, they were gone. So was Mrs. Jones and Mr. Jones and MaryAnne. Gone, as though they had never been there at all. But he didn't think much about their absence. In fact, he felt incredibly tired, his eyes heavy. A powerful yawn forced itself from his lips. Sluggishly, he slipped out from the chair and stumbled up the stairs to his bedroom, brushed his teeth, and nestled under the cool, comfortable comforter, curling up with his favorite stuffed animal. The blue monkey, the one he'd had since he was a child. Quickly, and without trouble, he fell to sleep.

He never awoke again. At least, not fully.

Trigger warning: child sexual assault

Memories of It

After I told her, my mother, blank-faced and trembling, rose from the couch and fumbled for her phone. She called my dad. "H-hi," she said when he answered on the third ring, one hand pressed over her lips. "Can you come home?" She was quiet for a moment. "Yes, now."

. . . .

I'm not sure when it first began. In fact, I don't remember a time when it wasn't happening. The earliest memory I have of it, of his hands trailing my back, slipping under my shirt, under my pants, his wet lips on my ear, on my closed mouth, the smell of cigars and leather overwhelming my senses and lingering on my sheets, was when I was six. Being that young, I hadn't yet received a warning for something like this. I had been taught stranger danger, of course, but this was no stranger. This was my grandfather, so what was happening was okay. *Right?*

I don't want to talk about him any longer.

. . . .

The CPS office was cold and stale. It was a few days after I told my mom, after my mom told my dad.

They took us back, my parents to one room, me to another.

"How long has this been going on for?" the woman asked me.

"I'm not sure," I told her. "Seven years. Maybe more."

She nodded. Wrote something down.

I don't remember much of what I said after this. I think I've mostly blurred it out. But I remember that my parents and I went to IHOP afterwards. I ordered chocolate chip pancakes and orange juice. I remember making jokes, smiling a lot, laughing about something that had occurred in school last week. I did that a lot when moments were tense, and to my knowledge, I still do; mutter something funny, grin, when I talk about hard things. I smile, all the time, when I'm trying to ignore something troubling me.

Or when I'm trying to forget entirely.

. . . .

I won't forget this.

"Can you give me a kiss?"

The one question I was asked, every time. It haunts me now. Such a trivial phrase, yet it remains hanging in the back of my mind like a dark cloud, my chest tight the very moment it is brought to my awareness. I can no longer be asked this phrase, at least not now. Not yet. Because with this phrase, it came, and I would lie, so still, until it was over.

That is, until I said "no". He froze, hesitating, unsure of what to do. And so, I rose up, and I stared at him, hard in the eyes, and I said it again. Stern, yet my voice trembled along the edges like a sturdy vase on the verge of shattering..

"*No.*"

He left, hurriedly, and he never touched me again.

. . . .

One night, my grandmother and I sat in the living room with steaming cups of tea. I told her about the book I was writing, and she told me she knew I'd become a fabulous writer, had always known since I was young. I still remember her face, pudgy and round, small eyes behind thin frames, shoulder-length dirty blonde hair always half-up. I remember her smell, clean and salty, like the smell of the beach at dawn. I found a candle that smelled exactly like her once and cried when I did, cradling it like a child. I lit it only occasionally and savored each time I did so. I haven't found a candle quite like this since.

The last time I saw her, I didn't know it. She waved goodbye to me at the airport and shouted, "I'll see you very soon, my dear!"

I waved back, tears pressing forth when she disappeared among the crowds, my secret stored in the back of my mind, preparing to unleash. And I hadn't the slightest idea.

I dream of her sometimes. Of her taking me to the Disney store, letting me pick out whatever I want, just like she did when I was younger, when I was still innocent, when I didn't know that what was happening was a bad thing. I dream of her swooping me up in her arms and forgiving me, loving me.

. . . .

I've never written about this before. Any of it. Perhaps it is because it is the most vulnerable thing that has ever happened to me, and I don't want anyone to feel bad for me.

Compassion is the last thing I want.

The wall, it builds around me. It has never really stopped growing, thickening, razor-sharp swords extending out from every direction. No one can hurt me, ever again, now that I'm safe behind this wall.

But I know now that this is not true. Not entirely.

It is time for this wall to fall down, and it *is*, crumbling one stone, one sword at a time. This piece, this very one, is a start.

What I want is for people to find familiarity in my story, to find comfort knowing they are not alone. That you are not the only person who stayed awake at night, waiting for him. That you are not the only person who has had to heal, who sometimes feels at fault for it when that is hardly the case at all, who has been ignored, who has been used, who is now triggered by the slightest of touches, the smallest of words, the most insignificant of actions, who has had to say "no" louder, and louder still.

Okay. This is the last thing I will say about him.

When I was twelve, a few days after I said "no" for perhaps, the first time in my life, my grandfather entered my room and sat on the edge of my bed and without much hesitation, I stood, rigid, and curled into a ball in the corner of my room, avoiding his eyes. He never spoke, although he parted his lips, tried to say something, I think. Eventually, he left. And I have a good feeling that I know what he wanted to say, but didn't. Couldn't.

Coward.

. . . .

An endless collection of miniature Christmas buildings and houses, too-many reindeer. A playroom with a golfing arcade game and a table for Legos and puzzles. A tea factory. One week every summer, entirely planned out, from amusement parks to movie nights. Late afternoons spent sipping tea by the fire. Thanksgiving at my great-grandparents house, which smelled of wool and comfort-- I cannot explain it any better than this. Roosters, all over the kitchen. A tuned piano near a large window that overlooked a forest, deer trekking through from time to time. A jacuzzi bathtub that my sister and I overflowed with bubbles once, creating an absolute disaster. Late night Sonic milkshakes. My uncle's wedding, on the beach, dancing in an uncomfortable dress, missing my dad's speech to change clothes. One night, on the Fourth of

July, when me and all the men of my family lit fireworks deep into the night, screaming wildly as the sparks chased us around the park, nipping our heals. Cousins, great-grandparents. Family, a big one at that.

    Good memories are precious. I hold onto them, still, with all the strength I have left. Sometimes, they overpower the bad memories. Those are the best days.

Vortex

My job is to guard the vortex, which mysteriously appeared on earth a few years prior. Although the researchers have worked tirelessly, collecting samples, observing the sky and the stars, they haven't found any answers, nor even clues. Nothing at all, really; they've only stumbled upon more and more mystery. It'd probably help if they were closer to the vortex, but they never get close to the vortex. No one does. In the beginning, they sent a few men down into it, suspending them over the whirring purples and blues by a rope attached to a crane, and once they got close enough, barely dipping into it, still several feet above its center, they were wisped into the unknown, being whirled down into the darkness. More like pulled, or yanked, the robe having snapped in half, bending the crane slightly as it did. That was years ago, and none of them have returned. Therefore, we don't go near the vortex. None of us. Not even within ten miles of it--they say, those who originally were that close, in the forest, heard voices. Voices that spilled into their brain through the slit of their ears and coerced them, loved them, cared for them, then corrupted them, controlled them and led them straight into the abyss. This has happened to five people. One of them happened recently. They say he had gotten too close, but others claim he was eleven miles from the vortex. Therefore, there's talk of expanding the perimeter. The vortex is growing, they think. What this entails, we have no idea. I am only a guard, anyway. And besides, I doubt it's growing. How would something like that even enlarge?

But then again, how would something like the vortex even appear?

While on my sixteen-hour shift, my legs grow weak and my knees quiver under my weight, yet I remain tall. I have to--people, especially young teenagers, venture here all the time, making their journey through the thick marshes and hiding behind bushes and long-dead trees--everything natural within 30 miles died the moment the vortex appeared, including the people. I'm also the best eye they have. The children peer at us as we stand along the wall, and they think that we can't see them. We can--we heard them coming from ways away. We warn them once, and most of the time they don't listen, mostly just frozen with fear, shocked that they were spotted, as though the warning signs were only pranks, their eyes wide and dewy above the gray brush, and so we warn them again. At this warning, most of them run, but some don't. So, we warn them again. After that, we shoot them. We must. No one goes near the vortex. Not even us. A few hours ago, I shot an older man who had come with his grandson, I presume. The old man cursed at us, claimed we were hiding something dangerous, claimed people deserved to know what it was. I didn't want to do it, but he wouldn't stop. I nearly had to shoot his grandson, too, when the grandson was hesitant to run from his grandfather, who had collapsed into the pond and slowly sunk below. Thankfully, he obeyed, fleeing, but now is possibly without a caregiver. Foolish, selfish bastard, that old man.

A few hours later, I am off my shift, and join my shift mates for dinner in the cafeteria. Our meal is meatloaf, mashed potatoes, steamed vegetables, and a brownie for dessert. Oh, and a Coke Zero. I always have a Coke Zero.

"Did you hear? We lost another this afternoon," Jeremy says to me.

"Another?"

"Yes, another."

"Who?"

"Samantha."

"What? How? She's been here longer than us. She knows not to get close to the vortex."

Jeremey shrugs, takes a bite of his brownie before starting on his dinner. "She didn't. At least, that's what Caleb said. He saw her last night, walking mindlessly toward it, toward that big, purple monster."

"Damn."

"They say it's growing. Say we need to position further out."

"I've heard that, too. But I don't know if I truly believe that. I mean, *shit*, all I know is that it's been stagnant for years."

"We know nothing about it, John. We don't know what it can do."

He's right, and the idea of an expanding vortex frightens me to the core, although my face remains as sharp as stone. We don't show emotion here--we are tough, strong, mentally, and physically. We have to be. But I can't help but wonder, anyway. What would happen if it did continue expanding? Would it consume everything, in time? Feeling my throat tighten, I change the subject by sharing the incident with the grandfather and grandson with Jeremy.

"Bastard," Jeremy replies, shaking his head. He finally starts on his mashed potatoes. "What a selfish bastard." He's talking about the old man.

I'm lying in bed when I hear it. Soft, gentle, like delicate hands meticulously caressing my mind. "*John….*" It says. "*John… John… John… follow me.*"

I rise from my bunk, slip on a jacket over my boxers, and saunter outside. I hear someone calling to me from the bedroom, but I don't really hear it. I don't really hear anything. Or see anything, either. Only the distant, purple hue of the vortex, bright and beautiful and welcoming me toward it. It wants me to be a part of it. The voice, it wants me to be a part of everything, the land, the sky, the Universe, everything in between. I can almost taste it, the power I could potentially obtain.

I'm here, standing above it, and the large, gaping hole whirs, like transparent liquid. Its illuminance pulls toward me, clings to me, as the voice cries, "*John…John…. Come to me, come to us, John.*"

I'm falling. I don't know how I fall, but I do, but it doesn't feel like I'm falling. It feels like… I'm floating. My eyes open--I hadn't realized they were closed--and the colors are magnified, they're all around, and I feel my skin, my muscles, my organs, my bones... they begin to dissipate until I am nothing, until I am everything.

"*Welcome, John.*"

I am everything now. I am even God. I am even

you.

Do you see me?

Do you hear me?

Do you sense it? The whirring?

It's here.

Crimson Tie

My hand tightens around my glass, empty besides two ice cubes and a residue of scotch. *There's nothing to worry about*, I tell myself. *You're fine.* But I don't feel fine. My gut twists and the back of my neck moistens, the ice cubes clinking as my wrist trembles. I dip my chin, exhale a shaky breath. *Pull yourself together. You're at a party, after all.*

The English manor roars with life, well-dressed people sauntering around and catching up with old acquaintances that they haven't even briefly thought of since attending St. Victoria Academy twenty years prior. St. Victoria is a secluded private school for only the wealthiest of children in southern England. The women's lips are bright red as they chat among themselves in their best plunging necklines, the men glancing them up and down from opposite sides of the room as though they're frightened of the women, unsure of what to make of their new figures. Meanwhile, I stand in the shadows, observing, just as I did back then. No one really notices me, as usual. For once, this is ideal.

I inhale and the scent of rot and mildew penetrates my senses, and in response, my nose scrunches, and my forehead wrinkles. Following this, an all-too-familiar ear-splitting scream ricochets in my mind. My body spazzes at this and my eyes search the crowd frantically. The scream dissipates and the chatter levels. I breathe in deeply and find that the overpowering smell has vanished without a trace or the slightest residue. The rot was never there, I decide, and presumably, neither was the scream. *God, I'm going insane.*

I consider leaving early, yet decide against it, as I may more likely become a suspect. I need to stay here, seemingly enjoying myself. That way they'll look at me as just another alumni here for a grand time. So, I decide to fetch myself another scotch just to pass the time. I need something to calm me down, anyway.

My knees quake as I make my way to the bar, my tie awfully tight around my neck. Hopefully no one notices me move with such rigidness. But I doubt they will. At the bar, I nearly knock over a glass of champagne when my elbow twitches upon setting it down, and I apologize swiftly, keeping my eyes low and moving to the side. I'm terribly out of it this evening.

Just as I am handed my scotch, a voice that is seemingly still undergoing puberty in the way that it cracks calls, "Fred! Hey!"

My eyes flicker up to meet the eyes of Samuel, one of my closest friends at St. Victoria. He beams at me, approaching the bar in quite an awkward manner. He hasn't changed one bit, wearing an olive vest over a baby blue button-down--he always had the most dreadful style.

I nod at him, and he holds up a finger. "Don't move. One moment." He orders himself a gin and tonic, then skips over to me. "My *god*, it's good to see you!"

Smirking, I take a swig of my drink. *Everything is fine.* "And to you as well."

"So, how have you been?" he asks me. Although he looks the same, I notice the smile wrinkles that have been permanently carved into his hollow cheeks. And there's something slightly off about his stare; a flicker of excitement dances in his eyes, yet it's not directed toward me, but something else. He appears almost… *hungry.*

"Good," I reply. *Just enough, not too much.* "And you?"

"Oh, don't small-talk me. Give me the nitty-gritty. It's been twenty years, after all!" The bartender calls out his drink, and he grabs it, thanks the bartender generously, then motions us to a nearby corner beside the crackling fireplace. He seats himself in a loveseat and his legs carefully cross. "Go ahead, sit down. Let's catch up."

Hesitating, I stand next to the love seat opposite of him, biting hard on my bottom lip. He lifts an eyebrow, noticing my standoffishness. To not draw too much attention to my unusual demeanor, as I was fairly comfortable in my body and leaned into awkwardness in school, I sit, my foot tapping restlessly against the hardwood. The scent of rot returns then, causing me to gag, yet it fades just as suddenly as before. An emptiness settles in my gut, perhaps even a hint of worry. I think to myself, *Stay calm. We can't give him anything.*

"So, tell me," he says. "What work have you been doing?"

I take another swig of my scotch and fixate my eyes on the whipping tails of the fire, which are warm on my face, even from where I sit. "I, uh, took over my father's company four years ago after he unfortunately passed away."

"Yes, yes. I heard about that. My condolences to you and your family."

Without tearing my eyes from the fire, I smile coyly. "Thank you, Samuel." A sharp echo of laughter fills the room, the buzz of pleasantries lifting in volume alongside it then falling back down to a dull roar like an ocean wave.

"I will say, however--and please don't take offense to this--but I do find it rather odd, you know, the way your father passed. I didn't know your father was clumsy enough to fall down the stairs and hit his head hard enough to rupture his skull."

My chest tightens, my breath caught at the base of my throat. I try to swallow but find that my mouth is dry and filled with sand. My eyes dart to Samuel, just for a fleeting moment, long enough to catch the lift of his eyebrow, that flicker in his eyes. I turn my attention back to the fire and finally, I swallow. "Interesting of you to say to someone in grief."

"As I said: please take no offense. It was just an observation I had."

I don't respond for a moment, and neither does he. In all honesty, I was not expecting something like that to come from Samuel, as he is normally one to keep observations to himself. "He was drinking," I finally add. "You knew he was an alcoholic. He was bound to trip sooner or later."

Samuel nods once, like he understands now. "So, is that all you've been up to?" he goes on. The chattering and *clinking* looms around us like thick air. "Running your father's company?"

"Yes," I say shortly, lifting my scotch to my lips. "There was a woman in my life a year back but *luckily*, I'm a bachelor again." I chuckle, turn to him with a wide smile, hoping that maybe he'll drop it. *Please, drop it.* But his face remains a stone despite a sloppy smirk that hangs there.

"Yes, same here. Although, you know me. I've never been interested in women, really. Only school. Now, work. I find women to be a distraction." His smirk widens, then falls completely. He leans forward, elbows resting on his knees, his completely full gin and tonic resting between his palms. He looks at me deeply, and for once Samuel looks… *intimidating.* Hungrier. "Doesn't George work for your father's company?"

My smile loosens, my muscles now tense and the glass of scotch slipping through my grasp against the moisture of my palm. I tighten my grip hastily, but I remain calm. Mostly. "Yes, he does."

"Has that been fun? Working beside an old pal?"

"Oh, certainly," I say.

"We were best buds, weren't we? You, George and I. We had a bloody good friendship, didn't we?"

I force out a chuckle. "Yes indeed!" I catch a glance at my watch, which peeks out from beneath my navy-blue suit jacket. "Oh, wow, it's getting rather late."

He ignores me. "About five years back, George mentioned to me that your father offered *him* the company, not you. Is that so?" He tilts his head to one side, sipping his drink.

"Why all of these questions?" I ask him, but my words come out like a wheeze as my tie continues to tighten around my neck.

Samuel sits back in his chair, his frame frail against the width of it, and extends his legs. "Oh, you know. We haven't caught up, you and I, in such a long time. Just curious, is all."

I sit up a little straighter in my chair. "Alright. Well, I had a wonderful talk. I'm afraid I have to--"

"Have you seen George tonight?" he asks me. His stare hardens on me and his eyes narrow as though he is proposing a threat. His glass trembles as his fingers curl tighter around his glass.

The buzz of the chatter dims, blurs, like a watercolor painting around us, my heartbeat now loud and prominent, the only thing I can hear. My eyes bore into the eyes of the man I once knew as friendly, charismatic, likeable to all. Now he is cold, bitter, and continues to press on.

"I have not," I respond, keeping my voice low and *normal*.

"Neither have I. And the party began--what?--two hours ago?"

"Yes."

Samuel glances around, as though searching for him. "*Hmp*," he grunts, shaking his head. "It's so peculiar, because just this afternoon, an hour before the reunion, he told me he was on his way. And now, he's not answering his phone. Either he's ignoring me, or something has gone wrong. I can't imagine why he'd be ignoring me, though."

His eyes sweep back to meet mine. "I'm not sure if you knew this, but George and I have remained good friends. In fact, we've spoken nearly every day since high school. Did you know that?"

My mind clouds with racing worries and probabilities. *Does he know? He can't know.* I shift in my seat, remembering where the nearest exit is, planning my swift escape. How I'll leave without him noticing, however, I have no idea.

"I did not," I say, a grin emerging onto my face. "How nice."

"Yes, nice indeed." He smiles, lifting his drink to his lips and taking a long, deep gulp, finishing it off entirely, then setting it down on the floor. "He told me a lot about you," he says as he sits back up in his chair, looking me in the eye with a darkened stare. "About how much you hated him."

"I--"

"There's no need to explain, Fred. You've always hated George, ever since Year 10. There was just something about him that irked you beyond belief." He shrugs, drifting his gaze to the fire. "I always assumed it was because of the way your father loved him and treated him like a second son. I know how much that bothered you."

Heat crawls up my throat and rattles me to the bone. "That's enough, Samuel. There's no need--"

"I mean," he goes on, amusing himself, "he chose George over *you* to run his company." His eyes flicker to mine. "Did that not frustrate you beyond belief?"

"Samuel, I'd rather not discuss this anymore." George's eyes, wide and panicked and *pathetic* flash in my mind, and I tremble at the sight.

"You know," he presses, snickering to himself, "sometimes I wondered if you were out to get him. The way George would speak of you... I think he was afraid of you."

I scoff. "As *if*. You know me, Samuel. I've never hated anyone. In fact, George and I also remained close after high school. I mean, we *worked* together."

"Oh really? You don't seem too close. I mean, at least from what George tells me."

My eyebrows furrow. "Are you trying to get a rise out of me? What the *hell*, Samuel?"

His sloppy smirk returns as he shakes his head. "Oh, Fred. You poor thing."

"That's *enough*," I growl. "I have to go." I begin rising out of my chair, my legs weak.

"I know what you did."

My heartbeat skips a beat, the sand returning to my mouth. I look at him. "What are you talking about?"

Chuckling, he says, "You didn't even care to clean the blood from your tie."

I dip my chin down, and there in the center of my tie is a faint but deeply crimson splatter across the white canvas. "That's not--"

"I know what you did. I know everything. You killed your father four years ago to stop George from taking the company, and two days ago, George figured it out. After some digging, he found evidence--your father didn't die from falling down the stairs; someone struck him on the head---"

"That's not true!" I interrupt.

"The medical records prove it," he spats. "But someone figured out a way to cover it up. And you didn't think George would tell me what he found, being his closest friend? Oh, poor, poor thing indeed. I know what you did, Samuel. There's no escaping the damage you've done."

"You know *nothing*," I snap. "You shut your bloody mouth, Samuel. Or I'll shut it for you."

He scoffs. "Ha! You think you can intimidate me? It's too late, Samuel. And, do you know what's funny? I can't seem to find George tonight. It seems as though--"

"I did *not* kill him! Nor my father!" Abruptly, I rise from my chair, my scotch falling my grasp and shattering against the hardwood. The room hushes, although I barely notice. All I notice is the heat, the blur of my vision, the nausea that intensifies.

"Hold your tongue until you get a lawyer," Samuel says.

"Wha--"

I am interrupted by the blaring sirens in the distance. They increase in volume quickly, shrieking wildly into the night, just outside the manor. The red and blue lights illuminate into the manor, coating everything in a horrifying and quite abrupt glow.

"Sorry, Fred. I had to."

I look down at him, and he smiles up at me, and before I can say anything else, my legs leave without me, racing out of the room at full speed. I bump into a few people, apologize briefly, but they don't say anything. In fact, they move out of the way, clutching onto their drinks, *confused* rather than upset. I doubt they even knew who I was.

Sister of Sleep

When I was a child, I killed insects, drowned them, crunched them, picked them apart. I'd spend hours in the backyard pouring buckets of water over ant piles, watching the way the dirt absorbed the water and turned to mush around my feet. The ants would scatter, and as they did, I'd pour water onto them as well, and I'd laugh proudly as though I had accomplished something.

One summer at the beach, my cousin stepped on a crab, killing it swiftly, and while my family played in the ocean, I took the crab apart, one by one, never once taking into account that the crab was dead, only completely mesmerized by its interior.

Further down the road, the act of killing seemed incredibly impossible to me when my cat was found flattened on the road behind our house. My dear friend's life was taken several years too soon, and for a while, I couldn't process it. I didn't want to. Even at twelve, I was angry at the idea of death, angry at its unfairness, it's inevitability. All my life I had been fascinated with act of dying and then it seemed I became desperate to prevent it. Tears would form at the sight of roadkill of any kind and sometimes resulted in me lying in bed for the remainder of the day, and when my friends sprayed chemicals on bugs that had crawled into our apartment, the sight of them drowning in poisonous puddles clenched my gut and at times caused me to uncontrollably sob. Recently, a roach peered at me from behind a bottle of shampoo while I was showering, and I killed it swiftly, and then I prayed. Prayed that he went to Heaven, or somewhere, prayed for forgiveness. It feels silly, almost foolish, but I suppose I do this because I now know the importance of life, after I had seen it taken, as though meaningless. Any life, regardless of how small, is a miracle. And I hate to be the person that takes that life away, any life, as it's not mine to take.

I remember one night, last summer, I felt incredibly existential. I lied in bed, thinking of how small I was, how temporary this life is. How time continues to tick by, how down the road, I will have my last kiss, my last breath, my last laugh… write my last piece. How terrifying such thoughts are. How frustrating. I'd pound my fists into my pillow, cursing God or The Universe or whomever, asking, How dare you give me such a short time? Such a minor *taste* of all of this pain, this wonderfulness, only to take it away?

Oftentimes when I find myself slipping into these existential dreads, as I still often do, I return to my Spirituality. Nose-deep in books, crystals spread around me on the floor, healing frequencies humming softly in the background, I soak up all the wisdom, all the hope I can. And it helps, it does, but only until the realist in me bounces back with logic. I've learned that while we can cling to hope, all we truly have is this very moment, right now, straight ahead and all around and so I breathe it in, all of it, and miraculously, this very moment is always enough.

Overtime, I like to say that I've met my internal dread in the middle; I've somewhat come to terms with death, with the fact that everything dies and trying to prevent it won't fix anything, really. It'll just make you mad. Trust me, I made myself go *terribly* mad. One might say that now, in this moment, I find death beautiful. A part of life, just like being born. That's all it is, really.

The thing that calms me down most, when I slip deep into my head, is trying to remember what it felt like to be in the womb. Remembering what it felt like before I was born.

And when I can't, I feel comforted, somehow.

I also like to wonder what it feels like to be asleep and to dream of nothing.

And I cannot.

On my walk to class, there lies a decaying squirrel in the grass. When I first saw it, I stopped and stared at it, blank-faced, noticing it's missing eyeballs and sunken body. For some reason, I didn't find the squirrel grotesque in the slightest. I found it natural, almost lovely. Especially when later that day, a different squirrel leapt across the sidewalk in front of me, and I couldn't help but think: *Although everything dies, everything is also born. Life is always continuing. And death awaits all of us. In time, when we are ready, when the world has decided we have completed what needs to be done, we will be one with the earth.*

This, to me, is what makes life so valuable, and what makes death not an end, but a connection. A rest. The act of morphing into the very earth that brought us

life. Of lying down to rest, and never truly waking, but knowing that you have lived. *Did you hear that?*
　　You lived.

No More Real Than Water

I'm not human. I never was. In fact, none of us truly are—we are mere illusions, existing through our own eyes, through our own minds. This world we see is not really there, just tricks of light and images our brains turn to something meaningful and dimensional. I think about these thoughts often, each time I ponder on my past and who I used to be. I thought I knew what life was, only to be wildly mistaken, slapped in the face by occurrences that not even science, not even God, could explain.

The rain pitter-patters on the window near my rocking chair. I feel my body sway with each dip of the heels, but don't move much else. I hardly breathe. They think I'm insane here, and I don't blame them—I twitch often, and my words are only whispers and wet coughs. A nurse watches me now from across the room. She's young, with a gold, cross necklace resting on her collarbone and her features are soft. She smiles at me now and again, her teeth pearly white and her eyes bright with tenderness. But I know she pities me.

Eventually, she leaves, and I'm left to admire the rain and its gentleness, despite the harsh winds that sweep it in all directions. The droplets trace sharp movements, but their sound against the glass calms my racing mind. For just a few moments, I can focus on something else. Although, I can't help but eventually remind myself that it's not real. The wind isn't real. Water isn't real. And I, despite my old age and heavy, limited movements, and seemingly realness of me, am not any more real than the nurse, or the water, or anything else.

And I am okay with that. With the idea of not existing. Perhaps, that is why I am here.

You. You believe you are real, don't you?

Then tell me. Where do you go, when you die?

The White Room

    I wake up. I'm in a room. The walls are white, the floor is white, and I am dressed in a white nightgown that falls to my knees. I am standing, but in front of me is a white chair. My fingers trace over the barren walls beside me, looking for a crack, any hint of a door, but there are none. And so, my gaze turns to the chair, and I make my way toward it, carefully, cautiously. I slide into it, my body fitting into its crevice quite perfectly. Behind me, I hear a projector turn, grumble, and click. Before me, there brandishes a bright, white light that materializes into an image. No, a video.

    It's me. I'm an infant, being born. I am small, helpless, gooey and sticky with juices, and am screaming wildly into the air. I watch the video, confused, but also, I am not just watching it, I am *there*. I am the baby in the video. I feel the doctor's glove beneath my soft back and the blinding light above my head shines quite violently into my eyes--it is all I can see. I am breathing. Oh, how bizarre it feels, to be born. How strangely new to me, despite the fact that I've been through it before.

    I am back in my seat, but then again I've never really left, and the video changes, fading into another video of myself but this time I am a child, barely walking, stumbling around on the grass outside as a woman with blonde hair, my mother, snaps photos of me while knelt down in the dirt. She's laughing, her smile wide and full. I feel the air on my cheeks and it was at this exact moment when my admiration for the outdoors blossomed, the crisp, fall smells, the sounds of the birds, the sway of the trees, the hum of the Earth beneath my stubby feet. The worms in the dirt, the little birds that sing and swoop down, the coyotes that cry at night, in the distance, far away. I collapse onto the ground and my mother races over to me, stroking my wispy hair, asking if I am alright but I am laughing, giggling maddingly. And so, my mother begins laughing too, planting a sweet kiss on my forehead. "I love you," she whispers in my ear.

    I am older, nine, maybe, and I am on stage, singing to some country song, wearing my mother's cowgirl boots, in front of the entire school. I'm rather bad, but that doesn't matter, not at this age. I'm trembling, my heartbeat quick at the base of my throat, my voice quaking against each note, especially the high ones, and the microphone slips between my sweaty grasp, and so my fingers curl tighter. When I'm done, after my throat has been rubbed raw, the crowd cheers ferociously, and my teachers high-five me, and I know I will be a singer when I grow up. I don't become a singer, but that's okay.

    My first crush, Steve Johnson. His hair, curled and crazed, round frames settled on a small nose, sharp jaw and lanky frame, exactly my type. I dip my head, walk past him, but as I do, he stops me, calls out my name. I forget everything in that moment, including where I was even walking toward at all--all that consumes my mind is his high-pitched voice, not yet greeted by puberty, and his acknowledgment of me. I stiffen, turn to face him, and smile. My cheeks flush with warmth, the back of my neck beading with sweat. He asks me what grade I got on my homework, and stuttering, I tell him. An A, like usual. But I don't say "like usual" out loud, of course. He also got an A. Then, he asks me on a date, and I say yes. Of course, I say yes.

A few months later, my first kiss, sitting on Steve's family's front porch, mugs of hot cocoa with mini marshmallows in them clamped between our palms, a cold night in late December, the air chilly, so we snuggle closer together. He smells of strong cologne and cinnamon sugar. His lips are soft, sliding across mine like butter. Christmas music hums from inside the house, the lights on the tree flickering, dazzling.

My approaching SAT test, the nerves that came with it, the late nights mindlessly eating my mother's "hidden" stash of ginger chews. Trembling fingers, rising nausea, making a friend while waiting for the test to begin in that stale, cold classroom, my stomach empty because I didn't eat breakfast. Passing the test, celebrating with my family at a local hibachi restaurant. I order buttery fried rice and soft, plump scallops.

I'm graduating high school. Our families are taking photos of us in our black gowns and matching jeweled caps. He is holding me tight, staring down into my eyes, and I am in love with him. But I cannot ignore the swelling guilt that forms in my gut as I wonder what comes next, with us going to different schools? I trust, to the best of my ability, that it will all work out. Love always wins.

My first heartbreak. My first real betrayal. Sitting on the curb outside my dorm at midnight, bawling into tight fists, shuddering against the pain. The loneliness. The dates, the mistakes, that came after. But the wisdom that came after those. The stories I could now tell.

Girl friends from my class, taking me out shopping, getting our nails done together. Late nights drinking tart, red wine before we were old enough and feeling rebellious, cool. Standing on the rooftops at night, overlooking the campus and the lights that glimmered, dotted along the buildings, and feeling infinite. Life felt so large, so untouched by my fingers, my eyes.

Graduating college, moving across the country to Washington. Oh, how time flies, I think to myself. The late nights studying in the campus libraries, never-ending projects and papers. The growth, the lessons learned. It all wisped by, in the blink of an eye. I've changed so much, even cut my hair. I remember that haircut, the bob with the blue ends and the long, straight bangs. I walk into my new job, on my first day, in my new, pressed gray suit, feeling powerful. Feeling myself, at last.

The day I ran into him, at the coffee shop down the street from my office. His red hair, dazzling green eyes, dark, chilled laugh, witty humor. Instantly, I knew. I've learned that when you meet them, your person, you just know. And I did. I watch us, hand-in-hand, strolling the alleyways after a romantic dinner, him pressing me against a building in an alleyway, but not in a violent sort of way, but in a passionate sort of way, because he also knew. It was so strange, that we both sort of... *knew*. Like two lost souls, finally connected, reunited. I want to dive into his skin and become a part of him. It was like we belonged in this world only at each other's side. A perfect balance. He drew back his lips and asked if we could go back to his place. Giddy, that's how I felt, when I told him "yes". I found love again, and it filled me, flooded me with meaning.

Walking down the aisle, toward him, my mother snapping photos with that wide smile on her face, tears brimming her eyes. My girlfriends, now bridesmaids, cheering and wooing wildly. My father is clutching my arm, tighter. He doesn't want to let me go. No, not yet. I'm kissing him, my husband, Jeff White. My last name is White, now. It's official. I belong to another person, and another person belongs to me.

We have three kids together, each one a year apart. Alice, Emma, and Walter. I watch myself give birth to all of them. I *am* giving birth to all of them, staring down into their eyes for the first time all over again. Giving new life, my superpower. I watch them grow up, slowly, but oh, so fast. I snap photos of them as they stumble around in the dewy grass, sit with them when they tell me about their first love, their first kiss, hold them during their first heartbreak, watch them as they learn and grow, fall and rise. My little humans, that I helped create.

This life, is slips by, flashing before my eyes, fading to black, then changing to something else, another experience, another moment, another person, another time. And all I can do is stare, living all over again, one last time. Date nights at too expensive places, us laughing about the cost. Oh, how he always made me laugh. Returning to work as an English teacher after having stayed home with the kids and loving every moment of it, changing one small life at a time. Getting lost in books, in stories, but never writing my own. But that's okay. Losing my mother, and soon after my father, resting by their grave, Jeff's arm draped over my shoulder, feeling my parent's presence waft over me like waves of golden light--they never really left me. At least, not fully. Traveling to gorgeous places, hiking through mountains and valleys, returning to my true first love, nature, that brief time when Jeff and I got into swimming and joined an adult group at a gym. When he and I also tried renovating a house but failed miserably. My college friends and I revisit that rooftop, overlooking the world, feeling infinite. Free. Young again, sipping from cheap bottles of wine and undergoing horrendous headaches that bleed into the next day. It feels like forever, it really does. It feels like it'll never end, this perfect little life of my own.

    In time, it dims. It always does, and it always will. Me, lying in bed, my husband, my children, staring down at me, crying. But I tell them not to cry. I tell them to enjoy this life. This precious, little life. I tell them to remember the moments, the heartbreaks, every loss, every victory, but most of all, the people. The connections. The life we've lived, and the ones that helped us live it.

    I'm holding Jeff's hand with the strength I have left, until it dissipates, and I am back in the white chair, in the white room, and the video fades, one last time, to black.

Part 2

Simply, At Rest

Coyote

Achak cradled the wounded coyote in his worn, chapped palms, a figurative knife digging into his gut and limiting his capability to breathe. He stared down into the dog's wide, black eyes and in that moment, he wanted to save her. But the wound was too deep, and anyone, near or far, could see that. The blood gushed out onto Achak's arms, mixing with the dirt and grime, which was powdered along his brown skin.

Achak was used to death. He experienced it often, but he couldn't bear it any longer.

His blackened fingernails dug into the coyote's coat, and he felt her chest rise and fall against his knees. "Shhh," Achak breathed, stroking the coyote's snout. This seemed to calm her, and for a mere second, her breathing balanced. But then, a high-pitched whimper escaped her black lips, her sharp fangs bared against them, and once again she was panicking.

"Achak," Nikan called from behind. His voice was carried off by the wind, and Achak stiffened, pulling the coyote closer to his chest, like only he was permitted to see her.

Nikan stood at Achak's side, panting and peering down at the dying coyote, who looked like nothing but a bloody blanket from where Nikan stood. It was obvious Nikan didn't know what he was looking at, and in response to this, Achak felt even worse.

Achak glanced up at his brother, catching a glimpse of Nikan's long, black hair, which was crazed and had been pulled half-up with a red feather. Nikan was a strong man, with broad shoulders and a stern expression that had been carved into his face at birth. Achak was not as durable as his brother, with a small figure, thin face, and black hair that was always up in a tight knot. He greatly disliked the hair in his eyes.

Nikan was twenty-three, and older than Achak by six years. Achak once looked up to Nikan, but once Mother was passed on to the spirits, and Noshi became a different man, shaping Nikan into a killer, Achak was forced to look at them both like prey would to a predator.

Noshi wanted them both to be tough--he was their father, after all. But, Achak had failed his father. Day after day, at each rising sun, Noshi reminded his son, Achak, that his brother, Nikan, was stronger, faster, a swifter hunter, and overall, a better son.

The words once stung, but then became nothing but a conjoined numbness. Such words became normal and ensured Achak that his life hadn't changed.

"Achak," Nikan repeated in a softer voice, crouching low to the earth beside his brother. He gestured to the coyote. "What is this?"

Nikan reached his dark fingers out toward the dog, which caused Achak to flinch away, baring his teeth, similarly to the coyote herself.

Nikan furrowed his eyebrows at this, leaning back in defense. "Achak?" Nikan glanced back down at the dog, staring at her cautiously through Achak's arms. "Is that--"

"*Ha:csonkonay,*" Achak barked in reply. "Yes."

Nikan became tense, his dark eyes hardening. "It cannot be," he said.

Achak closed his eyes and breathed in deep, petting the coyote's back and playing with her soft, brown-and-white-patterned fur. She was beautiful, as beautiful as anything else, and maybe even more so, too. She did not deserve to die.

Nothing deserved to die in Achak's mind, and this is what differentiated him from most—fearing death is what made him "frail".

"Did you do this, Achak?"

Achak's eyes tore open, and he jerked his head around to glare at his brother. Unintentional tears formed along the brims of his eyes, and although Achak willed them not to fall, he was not strong enough in this moment. "How dare you say such a thing?" Achak wailed, his vision now blurred, his lungs filled with a fuzzy heat, a sharp bitterness clawing at his throat.

Nikan raised his hands in defense. "Achak, I apologize," he said. "How am I to know?"

Achak withdrew his hand from the coyote's chest, revealing her wound, as well as her face. Once again, he stared deep into her eyes, but this time it was different… it caused Achak to somehow blame himself for this tragic happening and seeing her so afraid…. It was almost like he was looking at his own reflection.

"Who could have done this?" Achak whimpered, pressing a bloody palm to the coyote's cheek. "An animal would have eaten her... a Tonkawa wouldn't dare."

"And who would be so scorn as to leave her suffering, without even giving her life the least bit of appreciation?" Nikan snarled, leaning in to get a closer look at the dog. "Why would anyone leave her?"

"I don't know," Achak replied mournfully, at last tearing his gaze from the coyote, for he could no longer look at her. "I do not know what to do, Nikan." Achak turned to his brother, whose figure had slouched. "Nikan," he said. "You always know what to do."

Nikan shook his head in defiance. "Not now, Achak."

Achak bit down on his lip to press back his current aggravation.

"Father could help," Nikan said, glancing away from both Achak and the coyote, his black hair falling over his eyes and hiding his squared face, which had softened.

"Noshi isn't here," Achak snapped. It was no surprise that Achak called his father by his first name. Achak had resented calling him 'Father' ever since Mother died; he was no longer a fatherly figure in Achak's eyes.

Noshi had abandoned Achak, strengthening the better son, Nikan, and never second-glancing at Achak. And for that, Achak promised his own self that he would never forgive him.

But this was not the right moment to contemplate such thoughts—Achak was holding a half-dead coyote in his arms, and nothing else mattered besides this.

"Maybe we can save her," Achak said, lifting his chin and peering deep into the horizon. The green fields were endless, the sun slowly nearing the Earth, its rays creating a soft glow over the lands. The land was mostly flat, despite the few rising hills behind them. Achak's favorite spot was on a hill, which was a short walk from their village and overlooked the land in a way no other place did.

But this spot was good, too.

"How?" Nikan asked. His voice was low and quiet, and Nikan did not seem like himself.

Achak looked back down at the coyote, whose eyes were now limply closed—Achak could tell she was trying very hard not to close them. She didn't have much longer, and Achak knew this. He felt his breath thicken, his dry eyes stinging, for the tears had disappeared.

"You don't have to leave just yet," Achak whimpered, now to the coyote.

Achak had said the exact same thing to Mother, while she lay on Noshi's favorite buffalo hide and held Achak's hand with her frail fingers. Achak had said those words to her, staring deep into her eyes, and he remembered so clearly that in response, Mother only shook her head and smiled.

"My son," she said to him in a raspy voice, "you are the bravest of them all."

But Achak knew he wasn't brave. He was weak, and small; Nikan was the brave son, and Achak was led to believe Mother was confused, and spoke to the wrong son.

"Achak," Nikan said, setting a hand on his brother's shoulders.

Achak turned his head slightly, peering at Nikan with narrowed eyes. He pulled the coyote close to him again, wrapping her up in his warm embrace, hoping to somehow keep her alive this way.

"You cannot save her."

These words dug deep into Achak's chest, causing him to quickly intake breath and stir anxiously on the grass. "I can try," he replied in a harsh tone.

Nikan frowned, his stern expression returning. "Mother didn't want you to try," he said. "And she wouldn't want you to try now."

"How do you say this? How can you speak for Mother?" Achak growled.

"I knew Mother well, Achak," Nikan said.

"I knew her better than all of you!" Achak erupted, his tear-streaked face becoming red with anger. "She was the only person who treated me like I mattered, Nikan, and you of all people should know that."

Nikan sent him a sympathetic look. "My brother, I care for you--"

"Do not lie to me, Nikan," Achak growled. "All you care about is making Noshi proud."

"You have never spoken this way, Achak."

This was true--Achak was always quiet, and he'd rather listen than speak. He blamed Noshi for his reserved personality, for Noshi was the one to compare Achak to dirt and encouraged him to keep his lips sealed.

Achak turned away from his brother, staring deep into the coyote's eyes. He stroked her neck, and she whimpered softly.

"Maybe because I've never had the opportunity," Achak admitted in a gentle voice.

"Why do you say this?"

"Noshi hates me."

"Father is mourning, Achak."

"And I am not?" Achak's eyes flickered to meet his brother's, and Achak noticed that his brother was now sitting comfortably on the grass, his legs crossed, his fingers pulling weeds from the earth.

Nikan didn't look at him. He sighed, then said, "Father does not try to--"

"I do not--"

"Do not interrupt me, Achak!" Nikan roared. Then, he cleared his throat. "*Father* does not try to hurt you, Achak. He is trying to make you stronger, only. Father loves you, Achak."

"Father does not love me."

"*Achak!*"

Achak's face wrinkled as he held back whatever fought within. Was it guilt, or sadness? Maybe it was both. At that point, Achak didn't know anymore. He held the coyote closer to his bare chest, feeling the pace of her breath decrease against his skin. *Please, do not go, Owner of the Earth.*

"Why do you not speak with Father about your feelings?" Nikan asked his brother, cocking his head to look at him.

Achak met his gaze, which was brilliant and outlined by the sun's light. "Father won't listen to me."

"Father will not listen until you speak, Achak."

Achak turned away from his brother's cold eyes, and now he was staring at the endless, green field. The sun was setting now, decorating the sky with streaks of orange and pink.

And the coyote was dying.

Achak was not ready. He did not want her to die, but there was no way he could save her, and he knew this now. Nature would take her at any moment, and in the afterlife, she would thrive. She would be at peace, and yet, Achak was afraid, because who is to truly know if her soul is safe?

Achak trusted the earth, and he trusted the sky, and he trusted the way of life, but the way of life remained increasingly difficult, and he seemed to be the only one suffering. He seemed to be the only one to question life's motives.

"I love you, Achak," Nikan said.

This startled Achak, and he didn't precisely know why. He looked at his brother beneath the glow of the setting sun. "And I love you, Nikan," he replied. As he said this, a wave of heat washed over him, and he shivered. A heavy stone lifted from within, allowing Achak's breath to become steady, and encouraging his thoughts to calm.

It was always a competition with Nikan, but, during this moment, Achak looked at his brother as a friend. He realized then that Nikan was never against Achak, and that all along, Nikan was by his side, guiding him.

Achak was holding onto the past so tightly, he failed to realize he still had a family.

"You are strong, Achak," Nikan went on, turning his eyes toward the sunset, which had now caused the sky above them to darken, an array of stars peering down at them. "And you are brave, just as Mother said."

"Why?" Achak whispered.

"Because, Achak, you are kind, and you are sincere, and you see what others do not."

"This makes me brave?"

"Even I wouldn't be so brave as to show a hint of kindness to anyone but you, or Father," Nikan said, smiling to himself.

"I am sorry, Nikan, for thinking of you and Noshi as my enemy." Achak breathed in deep, feeling the coyote's soft fur against his chest. "It was I who became silent and excused myself from the family."

Nikan patted his brother on the back but said nothing.

The coyote whimpered, which cut through the quiet, light air around them, and both Nikan and Achak glanced down at her.

"It is time to let her go, Achak," Nikan said, softly.

Achak closed his eyes and remembered Mother. He thought about her smile, and the way she wiped his tears away when he'd skin his knee fighting with Nikan, and the way she held him at night as the village huddled around fires and told ancient stories of the past. He grew up beside Mother, listening to tales of the powerful *Ha:csonkonay*.

He also grew up beside Noshi. Noshi taught him how to hunt, and fish, and how to be a man, not a boy. Noshi was there when Mother was not, which wasn't often, but often enough.

Noshi took care of Mother during her final days, and because of him, Mother seemed content with her death. She was not in pain, and she was not sad.

But even then, it was challenging to let her go, undoubtedly so.

Father is mourning, Nikan had said. *Father will not listen until you speak, Achak.*

Maybe it is time to speak to Noshi, Achak thought to himself, digging his fingers into the coyote's fur. *Maybe, I am brave.*

Achak felt the coyote stir in his lap, and when he opened his eyes to look at her, he noticed that her gaze was wide, and the blood from her wound had stopped flowing. He held her closely. "*Ha:csonkonay?*" he said.

And, to his surprise, she barked wildly into the night.

"It is *possible*?" Nikan said, pressing a hand to the coyote's cheek, which was now warm with a sudden liveliness.

Achak rose abruptly from the ground, holding the coyote close to his chest, and Nikan followed. Neither of them could believe the coyote was showing signs of life, and they couldn't determine whether it was a miracle, or entirely unreal.

A thought crept into Achak's mind, and he gazed up into the sky, which was now dark and speckled with millions of stars. He smiled, and thanked his Mother, who gazed down at him through the constellations.

Achak would never have to let go of Mother--that was not the point. Mother was still alive, and Mother was happy, and this was her way of letting him know, healing the Owner of the Earth.

"Achak?" Nikan said.

"Come on, my friend," Achak said to Nikan, beginning the long journey back home by turning and walking over the hill behind them. "Let us go back home. I think that maybe, Father can save her."

And so Nikan followed him.

I Am Here

I don't know who I am. I look at myself in the mirror and all I see is you. You're looking back with your deep brown eyes and arched eyebrows and caramel hair and you're smiling because you're so happy. You're so excited and thrilled about life, standing there in your floral shirt and your necklaces and scrunchies that sometimes bother you because when you wash your hands they get soaked and stay soaked for three hours. And you're hugging him and you're telling him you love him and you're laughing with her and you're so kind and quiet but you talk so much and so loud and you get nervous and think you're being too intense. And you're sitting at a computer, typing away and marketing some book that you wrote a long time ago when you were sad and lonely but you're not anymore and so you feel strange, holding these books in your arms. You cry sometimes and then you wipe away the tears and stand up and do some yoga or call him or watch a show or read a book and you do everything you can to distract yourself from what's truly going on inside your head. You know, but you don't want to know, but I see it. I've always seen it. The constant fear of being left out, of being abandoned, of being forgotten. Over the years you have developed this persona of yourself, have built this wall made of razor-sharp knives and thick stone and you need everyone to know that you are happy and excited about life and kind and empathetic and talented and creative and the thing is, deep down, you are an ordinary person, and it frightens you. Even now, you're writing this and you're afraid. Your past comes back to haunt you late at night and all you want to do is take off into space and float forevermore until someone finds you and explains to you what you really are. They will sit you down and look at you, really look at you and answer all of your questions. But that hasn't happened yet. You feel the warmth when you pray, a golden illuminance blanketing your skin, like an angelic hug, but nothing has happened. Your questions remain unanswered. And you're afraid of dying, all the time, of closing your eyes and never waking up, because that would entail that your life has been lived for no reason and that all these stories you've written are just pointless monologues and does life even exist or is it all inside your head? You sit on the bus, in the back, and observe all of the people and you wonder if you are the only one who has a universe inside your mind, a universe so vast and daunting that you will probably never venture past the first star. And people love you, they love you so much, and you love them back but you don't because you don't know how to love, you're afraid to feel because when you feel, you feel too much and that's when you collapse and it takes a few months to stand back up. And I'm looking at you, and you're laughing, and I want to be you. I press my hand to the glass and part my lips and I want you to finally see yourself, the real me. I am floating in this universe inside your head and I am reading all of your secrets and I know that there is so much more to you and I don't know how to tell you because you don't want to listen. If the wall falls, you'll get hurt again and again just like you used to and you can't let that happen, not anymore, because even years later your wounds are still deep and fresh and bleed sometimes. But I want you to know that you are okay, and you are so strong and I am here, and I will protect you. Maybe, if you took those walls down, you would be able to see inside and see me, standing here. I've always been here. You will get hurt but that's okay because you're human and you'll heal, and maybe, when you finally see inside you can heal your other wounds, too. Maybe life *will* end and you will die but that's not a bad thing at all. Not at all. Because you lived, and you loved him, and you loved *them*, and you conquered the waves of your mind. You did what you wanted to do and you lived how you wanted to live and you were daring and authentic and imagine a world where you no longer had to smile your way through life—you can be yourself. You can just be, *you*. And you will be loved, anyway. I hope you understand that I will always—

Wow. That's enough writing time for today. I think I'll go to the gym and run this out!

Swimming

When I swim, it doesn't feel like I'm swimming. The water settles in my mouth like air--I don't notice it. I glide through the pool like I'm flying, my limbs outstretched, slicing through the water, although I don't feel the water, just an empty space encasing me in its embrace. It welcomes me home, the pool. I tilt my head to the right, breathe—I only ever tilt my head to the right, never the left. I suppose the left never quite stook, and the right feels most comfortable. I exhale from my nose and mouth in the form of bubbles followed by a soft moan I unintentionally make each time. One, two, three, four, breathe, two, three, four, flip, push off, glide, breathe, one, two, three, four, breathe. Over and over again. I could do it forever.

You don't have to think. Not when you're swimming. It's like walking, or running, but different from even those tasks--there's no sidewalk to mindlessly stare at, no fellow pedestrians or cars or tree branches waving in the breeze or loose pieces of trash gathered in bushes or snatched on branches. No squirrels, no birds, no distractions. Just you, the dark blue line on the pool floor that guides you, the T at the end—just as you pass, flip-turn-- and the vast blue all around. The best part is when your goggles fog and you can no longer see the blue, only a haze of the line, but you trust that your muscle memory knows the way, and it does. You feel infinite in this water, even though it's only a pool. This water is yours, wide and open, or at least feels like so.

You don't have to think. Not about swimming, at least, such as where you're going, how to breathe, how to flip-turn. But you do think, endlessly, about everything else. The awkward interaction you had with the barista earlier that day, your current favorite song ("Hey Kids" by Molina) playing on repeat in your head, your own private disco party in your mind, the fact that your old friends are going out to celebrate one of their birthdays tonight and you weren't invited but you aren't surprised—you haven't spoken to any of them in a year—and you wonder if you should text your old friend happy birthday. You wonder this for a long time, while you're swimming. You want to, but they probably hate you—I mean, they left you, so they most certainly hate you. Then again, your other friend, the one that's still part of the group and is still friends with you, assures you they don't hate you. They talk about you, quite often actually, but they don't hate you. At least, your friend doesn't think they do. This conversation makes your chest feel funny, but you nod and thank them for assuring you, and so you think about texting them happy birthday, and eventually, you do, and they respond right away and ask you how you've been and y'all catch up and you feel good—they don't hate you, they don't. You're still not invited. But you're not surprised. You probably wouldn't have invited them to your birthday party, either. And you don't.

You feel happy here. You can't explain it. A warm, fuzzy feeling creeps into your chest, and you recognize it as belonging. Being a part of something greater than yourself but something that doesn't require the same effort that writing does. It feels more natural, not that writing doesn't feel natural. But you're immersed in it to its entirety, literally, diving down to graze the bottom of the pool with your fingertips, rough on your skin, before pressing off to dolphin kick against the current you've made and emerge back up. Your entire body is moving, stretching, and you feel connected to yourself. For once, you love your body and the fact that it can swim, that it feels powerful while doing so. Yet beyond that, it's more than even love, more than connection. It's the feeling of simply being. *Being,* and that being enough.

    You're still swimming. Your arms are aching, your chest tight, and your nose is clogged with water, yet you hardly notice it at all. You're practically blind, but that's okay--you know where you're going. You've taken this path many times before, following the blue line, then not following it, only trusting, being, feeling. You're so far deep in your head at this point that you forget you're swimming at all. It's like driving, but more relaxed, less dangerous. When you wake up from your ten-minute-long trance and tighten your grip on the steering wheel and get a feel of where you are because you honestly don't remember how you got there and how you're still alive. Or is it *more* dangerous? You remember that you could drown right now, if you forgot to breathe, if you forgot how to move, if you decided to sink. You don't though. Of course, you don't. You've swam this path before, you know what to do.

But even so, sinking is one of my favorite things to do. In between sets I float to the bottom of the pool, the very bottom, and I rest there for a while. I can't breathe, and my lungs tighten and my chest swells, but I like it. I like that I cannot do anything but observe. The light slashes through the water, creating pulsating fragments of illuminance even way down here. The water ripples around me, but otherwise remains still. It's so still, and so quiet. Even my thoughts hush, as if they know better, know not to disturb such a moment. When my lungs cannot take it any longer, I stay some more. I'm infatuated by this sort of silence, the kind you can only find if you're at the very bottom of a pool, in the center of a forest, in the deep abyss of your own mind. I soak it in, all of it, feeling the water seep into my skin as I absorb it, become it, and am entirely fluid like the space around me, existing with the pool rather than in it.

Then, I rise back up, pushing against the bottom of the pool and feeling myself blast off, becoming whole again. Inhaling a deep, full breath, I pant for a while, listening to the hum of the overhead AC, the fellow swimmers chatting about the completed set, the water splashing and lapping against nothing. And I say goodbye to my home, and I tell myself I'll return to the pool more often.

I don't. And I'm never certain as to why.

What A Lovely Day It Is

We are under a large oak tree on top of a hill. The valleys are green and glinting with sunlight, blooming bluebells reaching up from the swaying grass. There is a breeze, and although it is slight, it strokes my cheeks, licks at my tangled, blonde locks, and feels nice on my skin. My head is in his lap and he is grazing my bare arm with his fingers, which are rough but comforting all at once. I am looking up at him, admiring his sharp jaw, his bright, green eyes. He is staring out into the valley, grinning slightly. I realize that I love him. We have been together for only a few moments, but I love him, and I am afraid to tell him. The moment I saw him, he became my best friend, not that I had many friends to begin with.

"What a lovely day it is," he says, glancing down at me and widening his grin. "You're beautiful. I'm the luckiest man in the world to have a woman like you." His hand cups my jaw and he leans down, planting a sweet kiss on my cold lips.

When he pulls away, I beam up at him, my entire chest fluttering with vibrant orange and yellow and pink butterflies. My head rests in his lap and I feel the warmth of his palm against my shoulder, tracing my cheekbones. Sparks race through my veins at his touch, making me feel more alive than ever before. I've always dreamed of feeling this alive. It is a feeling I vaguely remember.

Before him, I was awfully lonely, and I was not myself. There was no way for me to fix it. I would lie still and wait, staring straight up into the darkness. There was no breeze. But he has brought me back to myself, made me feel whole again. And for that, I am forever grateful.

I love him, but do I tell him? As I stare out into the fields of green, which carry a subtle heartbeat that you can hear when you press your ear against the earth, I wonder why the phrase "I love you" is not something one should say upon just meeting someone. Yet, at the same time, I feel as if I have known him for longer than a few moments. Part of me feels like I've met him before. His smell, his touch… I realize how familiar it all is to me. I miss him. I want to tell him that I love him.

But maybe, if I tell him, he will be afraid of me. But perhaps not.

I breathe in deep, my eyes shifting to look up at him. He's already looking down at me, his eyes wide and bright. They soften and shrink when he notices the shift in my gaze.

"I love you," I whisper, loud enough for him and him alone to hear.

My soul trembles as I wait for him to respond. I have never been so vulnerable. And I watch as his smile vanishes, like a machine unplugged from its source of power. He blinks at me, and then he is lying me back down on the grass. He covers my eyes, but I can still see him as he turns his back to me and then disappears down the hill.

I am still lying beneath the large oak tree; my arms are folded across my chest and I smile up at the night sky as a rat scurries over my body and a pink butterfly lands on my head. Eventually, the butterfly leaves, yet other butterflies, other insects, return to land on me as well, burrowing deep into my forehead, in my arms. I stay there, under the tree, for a long while. I am sad, and I realize that I miss him. Love him. But I think I prefer this over the dark. The grass grows around me, through me, encasing my heart, my lungs, in its tender embrace. I feel the root of the oak tree nip at my spine, and I wait, patiently, until I will soon be one with the tree itself. I lie so still that to those who pass, it might appear I am only a log.

Ghosts of the Sea

I stare down at the dark abyss that is the ocean. I cannot see the exact line where the black sky kisses the horizon, stroking the waves ever so gently. All I can see is a navy hue sprouting from a not-so-evident source. It could be from the ocean; it could be from the sky. It could simply be sprouting from me.

I lean over the railing, my fingers clutching the auburn-colored wood. I can see the railing, speckles of salt scattered around my trembling hands, beneath the gentle, white illumination overhead. My body tilts forward, and then my head arches back, and I fall into the rhythm of the boat's rocking. Luckily enough, I am not one to obtain the unsettling symptoms of seasickness, and in a way, I quite enjoy the natural sway I currently experience--not that I have the slightest choice as to participating.

Back home, everything seems to be much too still.

I continue staring down over the railing. I was mistaken because it is not completely black. The waves are visible from all over, white hills lifting from the murky liquid and crashing down, their hisses soothing my raging thoughts, which have had yet to resign to slumber until this very moment.

I breathe in, watching these waves. The white tips of them scatter about the sides of the boat. It is silent for a moment, and then they appear, erupting into ultimate madness. This is what makes the boat rock and leap toward the sky, which in fact remains such an unnerving dark, despite the sprinkled stars emerging into view. If you stare into the black too long, you will end up in a cold place, wrapped in wasted whispers and branded ideals. So that is why I look at the waves, not the sky. If I do not focus on the white tips, I find myself going mad in the head.

The white tips of the waves, I notice, look like wary ghosts. They soar across the dark waters, which could be well-mistaken as the empty part of the galaxies above, the hidden sections. White bodies wave to me from below and then dissolve into a mist, which in turn flies up and coats my flushed cheeks and settles into my crazed hair.

The wind is powerful tonight.

I lift my eyes from the waves, at last, and I unwrap my white knuckles from the sea-salt-coated railing. I breathe in the dark abyss once more, enjoying the sensation of enduring merely with my breath, no longer my thoughts. There is nothing in this moment besides the rocking and the crashing, and my breath, which is white in the air, and then is nothing at all. It is as though I don't truly exist, as though I am not even here. I am one with the night, a ghost of the sea.

And then I turn and wander back inside.

A Strange Observation

Dear Richard,

    I've made a strange observation that I'd like to share with you.

    I decided to take the bus to work this morning. Before taking a seat, I glanced around to see that everyone had headphones stuffed deep into their ears and their eyes were low and heavy. Of course, I didn't look too much into this and wandered to a seat in the back where the light was dim and easy on the eyes. I pulled out a book, which I'm afraid I've already forgotten the name of, and I began reading on page 76, when I felt the strangest urge to glance up. When I did, I saw the people on the bus bobbing their heads and tapping their feet to music, I presume, and I found this quite humorous because everything was quiet besides the sound of the tires trailing against the concrete. I heard no music, only silence. The people were completely absorbed in the background noise that played from their headphones and I watched them.

    I started to wonder which songs they were listening to, if any at all, and began playing a game in my head. *She's listening to Christian music; he's listening to rap.* And that's when I met someone's eyes and we exchanged glances and she darted her eyes away, avoiding my stare. And I noticed that nobody was looking at each other, almost as if a human glance was something to fear. Most everyone had their phones out, their thumbs tapping against the illuminated screens that brightened their faces, texting people who could not see their expressions nor hear their music nor smell their scent nor taste the sweetness of the air around them. Hiding behind a technological mask, eyes glued to a piece of metal.

Others were reading, would get distracted every now and then and glance around for a bit like me at that moment. But they returned to their book quickly. The rest, who had no distraction other than the background noise, kept their eyes low, steering clear of everyone's blank expressions. Everyone was sheltering from the eyes of one another.

That's when I noticed a young girl with stickers on her water bottle and pins on her backpack and she kept both in her lap as if she were expecting people to understand her solely through these five Disney pins, three pins referring to coffee in some way, one pin that was just the face of a dog. Others that I didn't recognize. Her water bottle had a water bottle sticker on it, which made no sense to me. The rest of the stickers said the names of local shops and inappropriate words that I would rather not repeat in this letter. Her face looked so blank and yet so miserable and yet so normal, I couldn't figure out what she was feeling or thinking. It was incredibly difficult to decipher what music was playing from her headphones. All I gathered was that she liked Disney and drinking water and possibly had a dog. She was just like everyone else. While trying to be unique, she ended up being completely normal. It made me feel sad, Richard… how accidentally normal she was.

A navy blue was painted across the early morning sky, the moon fading but still evidently there. The weather was crisp, and everyone wore jackets and pants and sneakers and this wasn't anything out of the ordinary. But I began to realize, Richard, that everyone was dressed the same. They all wore those same clothes I've seen in the catalogs. They were completely identical, and it frightened me a little. The worst part was that they were all trying to be different, just like the girl. But they were the same. My left eye twitched, just as it does when I'm nervous. You remember how it does that, right?

Everything about this observation made me sad, Richard. Of course, you could argue that they were simply tired and didn't think much about their clothes upon dressing, but there was something off about it all.

I ended up missing my stop, staying there in the back of the bus beneath the dim light, my book clamped shut beneath my hands, dry from the harsh air of winter, and I watched strangers stumble on and off, eyes boring into the floor as they did, reverting their eyes from the ones that watched. Some of them smiled at the bus driver, but only some. The longer I sat there--hours, probably-- the more I began to discern that everyone had the same hair color, the same hairstyle, the same eye color, the same skin color. Floating, blank heads attached to limp bodies that carried themselves on and off this bus, which smelled slightly of body odor and mold but otherwise smelled quite nice. Like ghosts, they glided through the walls, faces devoid of expression, creeping out into the chilly air from cracks in the windows and barely shivering at all. Their pins glittered against the bright streetlamps and their much-too-similar clothes clung to their body and they let those things and their stickers and their text messages and their social media posts and their colorful background noise tell the story of their lives. They depended on these things for a sense of purpose. Their eyes were black holes that dug deep into their eye sockets and worms crawled out of them as though they were only corpses, already dead, already gone. It was terrifying, Richard, but I kept staring anyways. They paid no mind to me, like I wasn't even there. Maybe I wasn't. At that point, I had no idea. They lied face down on the floor of the bus and moaned and yet, they kept their headphones on. The earth began shaking, volcanoes erupting in the distance, the sky black nothingness, ash raining down. Then the seas rose and overtook us all. As the bus glided down the rushing river that consumed the city, they kept their headphones on, still avoiding my eyes. And I sat there, listening closely as the world around me collapsed in on itself. The hours and the days and the weeks and the months and the years combined into one long moment that contained no importance whatsoever other than the fact that I was there, and they were gone, stuck inside their heads, stuck inside their repetitive stories and stubbornness, stuck inside this world… with me.

    Eventually, I stepped off the bus and walked home. I realized soon enough that I'd retired from work nearly twenty years prior. Oh, how embarrassing! I had no reason to even get on the bus in the first place and had no reason to make such a bizarre observation. Yet, I'm glad I did, Richard. I'm glad I did, and I'm glad I was able to write about it to you, as I am old now, and my fingers are thin and tremble.

I wish you were there to see it, Richard. I miss you dearly. It's been awfully lonely without you. And I don't want to become accidentally normal. No, I don't want to be just another floating head.

Your loving mother,
    Margret

I Don't Remember Much

"Well, you see, I don't remember much. What I do remember is that we were dancing, and then I was running. When I came to consciousness, abruptly, my legs came to a stop, and my upper body jolted forward. My hands grasped my knees as my head rounded down and I wheezed, quick, shallow breaths that stung my lungs. My lips were coated in a fine layer of slime, and my neck, my forehead, my chest were all moist with sweat, my clothes clinging to me uncomfortably. When my breathing came to a moderately steady pace, I rose and wiped my forehead with the sleeve of my gray sweater. But this hardly helped as moments later, beads of sweat trailed down into my eyes.

"How long had I been running? I have no idea. Enough to the point that my legs trembled beneath me, barely able to hold my weight, and my vision blurred around me. I brought one foot forward in an attempt to keep running until I was safe, fully, but in doing so my body collapsed to the forest floor. My fists slammed down on my thighs as I grunted and cursed through my exhaustion, exasperated. My fingers curled around my leggings, grabbing at the material, and that's when I noticed a wetness. At first, I assumed it was more sweat. Carefully, I turned my hands over to see them caked red, fresh with blood, which dripped onto the ground, splattering along the orange and yellow leaves that laid all around me, peacefully. That moment, despite the lovely scenery, was hardly peaceful. My palms quaked as my chin dropped. I tried to make a sound, but nothing escaped. All that I could hear were my shaky wheezes, which had returned at the sight of the blood, and the soft birdsong alongside the rustle of leaves in the wind. I never remembered what happened. I'm not sure how I had forgotten. Perhaps I had blocked it out, as I've heard some people do. I waited for any recollection of the previous events, but none came. My eyes squeezed close, and the tears pressed their way through. They weren't sad tears. They weren't frightened tears. They certainly weren't happy. I'm not sure why I cried, really, but I remember it was partially because I didn't know how I had gotten to this point. I didn't know how to climb out of this hole I had created for myself. I wasn't even sure what had happened, and I certainly couldn't return to figure that out. I didn't know what to do, where to go. How does someone move on in a situation like this, you know?

"My blood-soaked hands curled in on themselves as my silent sobs continued to force themselves out, using up whatever energy I had left. I looked at my chipped, teal nail polish and remembered when I had painted my nails, giddy for the cabin trip. We were supposed to rekindle on this trip. Things were okay again, and they were supposed to stay okay. Just the night before, we were eating mashed potatoes loaded with butter alongside gorgeous grilled steaks in some fancy, red wine sauce. We danced to Frank Sinatra, tipsy on chardonnay, in our slippers. I remember looking at him in that moment, while we were dancing, and feeling so deeply in love that it hurt. You know, that sort of love that swells in your chest, limiting your capability to breathe. I remember forgiving him for everything he had ever done to me. I knew, in my heart, that everything would be okay. Stay okay. I would be safe here, with him.

"A bird chirped from the trees above and the sound jolted me out of my memories, which now only left an emptiness. I stood, wiped my hands on my leggings, which left a red stain on both them and my palms, and I sauntered forward. I'm not sure how I did it--how I kept walking. How, after everything that had happened, I kept moving forward, into the unknown, my cheeks tear-stained but my face otherwise remaining blank. Like stone, I floated onward into the forest. At one point, I remember passing by a cabin with a couple inside, dancing to Frank Sinatra, tipsy on wine, an elegant Christmas tree settled in the corner, wrapped presents crowding the floor. I kept walking. My breath, which had steadied, was white in the air and I shuddered against the sharp, crisp winds. I kept walking, deep into the night. Besides the cabin with the couple, I don't remember much of that walk. Finally, just as the sun began to rise in the distance, I arrived at a small town, and I washed my hands in the public bathroom just outside of the town's library, dabbing at my leggings, as well, and I called a cab. The cab driver drove me home, and when I got home, I packed a bag, and I ran away.

"Why did I run away? Well, I presume that is obvious, isn't it?

"Yes. That is all I remember. Honestly. He's okay,

right? Please tell me he's okay."

You're Not Real

"I can't do this anymore," he tells me once we're seated on a bench on a balcony that overlooks the university below. We're close to each other, yet I can't help but notice the emotional distance between us, thick like dark smoke, settling in my lungs like rocks. I had felt our distance for a while yet tried to ignore it because I didn't want to believe it. Such a fear couldn't be real, not with us and what we had. And yet, I felt it, and it *felt* so real.

The moonlight spills onto us, creating a spotlight for this moment. I fall silent for a long time, staring at my hands. Inhaling a shuddering breath, I whisper, "What do you mean?" I know what he means.

He avoids my eyes. "I'm sorry. I just... we're not right for each other. Not right now."

We've only been dating for two months, but he's my only friend in this new, unfamiliar place. I can't lose him, the only person I have.

But when I look at his face, emotionless, his fingers fidgety in his lap, his foot tapping restlessly, I realize he's already gone.

. . . .

You wake up to a scratchy whisper in your ear that moans, *did you think you could hide from me?* Your eyes peel open and look up at the woman hovering over you. Her face is sunken and carries a purple hue, her eyes two black stones, her smile stretched out too far across her face, strands of her black hair spilling over her sharp cheekbones. You can feel her, a dense, cold cloud flooding into your chest, weighing you down, and you can see her in front of you, just as clearly as you see your comforter, your bookshelf, your ceiling. One bony hand clutches your bicep, hard.

Your breathing hastens, and you can feel the sweat pooling beneath you as you gaze up into her undead, hungry expression. For several, everlasting moments you do nothing, thinking that this may be the end, until miraculously, you manage to squeak out, "You're not real." But you don't really believe this. You're not even sure why you said it, where it came from.

Your eyes clench closed, then open to reveal an empty bedroom, encased in blackness and a painfully loud silence that rings in your ears. It's 4:05 a.m. and you cannot fall back to sleep because you can still feel her grip on your bicep, invisible fingernails etching into your skin.

. . . .

They say sleep paralysis first occurs during one's early 20's. About 8% of people experience it in their lifetime. It is a state of waking, or falling asleep, in which you cannot move or speak, and some even experience hallucinations. They see, feel, hear things that aren't real, but *feel* real. And after having just been in REM sleep, your muscles have completely relaxed, resulting in an inability to move them. You cannot move, cannot speak, can only stare.

     A trigger of stress or lack of sleep, sleep paralysis sometimes causes your nightmares to project themselves into your room, into the space around you, but lasts no longer than a few minutes, diminishing into the shadows when your brain finally remembers what's real, and what's not. Sometimes, sleep paralysis is so severe it leads to insomnia, sometimes depression or anxiety.

     There is no cure to sleep paralysis other than getting proper rest, implementing relaxing rituals throughout the day, and simply, enduring.

     Researchers believe the reason we see such creepy things during sleep paralysis, such as witches, demons, monsters, or aliens, is since they are common scary characters in horror films. Our brains have learned that these things are frightening to us and therefore place them in our dreams like pawns in a game of chess, and your mind puts on a show.

     And sometimes, there's a little spill. Imagination bleeding into a brief lapse of reality.

. . . .

     I rise from the bench, walk away from him. My knees wobble, my soul *empty*, and I drop to the floor, sprawled out along the concrete. I do this as though it's the most natural thing to do. At first, I'm quiet, and then, although I try to contain them, the sobs erupt from somewhere deep inside the vast *emptiness*, and I wail into the night air. My palms press to my eyes and my head shakes furiously. I pray that when I wake up, it will go away. I pray that it's not real.

When I finally calm myself down, finally open my eyes, he's gone, and I'm alone, and I stay on the ground for a long time, my eyes tracing the stars above, the cold air biting at my bare skin. But I like it—it makes me feel real. The scratchy concrete under my head makes me feel grounded.

I didn't even hear him leave.

My chest swells with incomprehensible pain as I wonder if he was ever real. If perhaps, I was so lonely, I had just made him up those months prior. My imagination slipping into reality, fooling me, distracting me.

Perhaps that would be better. Him being just another spill.

. . . .

The first time you experienced sleep paralysis, the same woman stood at the edge of your bed and stared at you, her face a blank stone. Her long, black hair wisped around her skeletal face, her eye sockets hollow, her collar bones protruding from her purple chest, which was mostly hidden by a black robe that consumed her. Your eyes bored into hers for quite a long time. You then noticed that you were in your bedroom, but not *your* bedroom. The walls were purple (yours are white) and the windows were open and sharp gusts of wind swept into the room, and you felt it--you *felt* it--on your cheeks, in your hair, in your lungs.

You stayed there for a long time, feeling held down by an invisible force, staring at the woman in your room. That is, until you rose from the bed, jabbed your trembling finger at her chest, and cried, "You… Not… *Real…*" and she vanished as though she had never been there at all. The windows were closed, and the room was dark. It was the middle of the night. You are alone.

At night, you stare at the dark corners of your room and you find yourself waiting for her and so you tell yourself, *It's not real. She's not real. You're not real.*

. . . .

Others say sleep paralysis is just a scientific term for being haunted by an evil spirit or demon. Religious people, mostly. They claim that you are either living in the haunted space, or a disturbed spirit has clung to you and proceeds to follow you. At night, you are most vulnerable, and they reveal themselves to you. Other signs of haunting include random bruising or scratches (especially in three's) on your body after waking up, experiencing the feeling of someone watching you, various objects miraculously moving or disappearing, and the sensation of a cold gust of air washing over you throughout the day.

I've experienced all these things.

I like to call myself an empath. Hypersensitive. Aware of the slightest disruptions of feelings or energies. Sometimes at night, in the dark, eyes bore into my neck, and when I wake up, I have scratches traced along my sides, on my chest, sometimes alone but sometimes in three's, located in all the places covered by clothing. Sometimes I experience bruising, too, and although I'm clumsy, I cannot recall how or when I hit my forehead, my shin, nor my thigh on anything. If it manifested in a bruise so large, wouldn't I have remembered it?

Once, while I was alone in my living room, I heard a strange noise from the hallway, so jokingly I called out, "Reveal yourself, ghost." Moments later, a record that hung from my wall perfectly still for over a year fell and crashed to the floor.

I haven't done anything about this. Of course, besides waving burning sage throughout my apartment. Perhaps it's because I've become immune to haunting. Bewildering, frightening thoughts coming and going, leading me deep into a spiral, frightening me into the night, following me wherever I go. Past wounds, future worries, people I miss. I know it's not real and yet it haunts me anyway.

I told my friend about my sleep paralysis, as well as my theories of a ghost grabbing my attention, and her eyes widened, and her skin became very pale. She told me to pray to Jesus and ask for safety, and when I reminded her I wasn't really religious, she told me she didn't care. She told me I was in deep, deep danger.

So, I prayed.

I think it might have helped. At least a little.

. . . .

This is the part of the story I avoid telling.

In my mind, I like to believe that he wasn't real. But I know he *was* real, so I like to believe other things instead. That it wasn't my fault, at least not all of it. That our friendship never expanded into something more. That I wasn't his first kiss. That wherever he is, he still thinks of me and in a positive way only.

I follow him. I don't want to believe it's over, can't believe it's over. I rise from the concrete and numbly, eyes blurry and pulse racing, stumble back into the building and race down the stairs, and I see him. Head bowed, blonde hair draped over his icy blue eyes, hands in his pockets, he actually looks *sad*. But I don't care.

And so, I scream, "So, you expected to just *leave* me?"

He turns to stare at me, eyes widening in fear—I hate that he fears me in this moment. Other people stare, too, but I don't see them, not until later.

I walk up to him, stare deep into his eyes. "Can we talk about this more?"

"Brittney..."

"Please."

"I can't—"

"Please don't leave me." Thick tears pour down my cheeks, and the world begins to blur around me.

"Brittney, I don't love you. I'm sorry."

I don't realize what I've done until after it happens. My arms are outstretched and he's looking at me in shock and people have stood around us now, unsure of whether to get involved. I shoved him, hard. But it wasn't me who did it, it *wasn't*.

"What the hell is wrong with you?" He shouts.

"I'm sorry," I whisper. "I'm so sorry." When he begins to turn, I ask, "Can I walk back with you? Just one more time?"

So, we walk together in a bitter silence, the darkness keeping us far apart, our connection forever estranged. The boy I once knew, once loved, now a stranger, nothing but a distant memory. I soak it up regardless, every moment with him.

When we arrive at my dorm, he turns to me and says, "Goodbye, Brittney." He says it sincerely, like he doesn't want to say it, his eyes soft and his voice cracked along the edges. Or, perhaps this is just me, making up stories. Caught in more allusions.

I watch him disappear into the night, and I never see him again.

A week later, I text him. I apologize for what happened, for how I acted, and I offer to remain friends, and I thank him for everything.

He has still not replied to my text. It has been three years.

I like to believe that my text never went through, that he simply didn't see it. That I never sent it at all.

. . . .

The relationship continues to haunt you, although rarely, and most specifically that night. When you weren't you, but someone else, someone too far gone in their mind to understand what was happening. You've forgiven yourself though, you have, and you hope he has forgiven you, too.

Occasionally, though, you think of the fond times as well. When y'all walked all the way to Victory Hall only to realize it was closed and y'all laughed until your bellies ached and y'all befriended a stray cat and then drove to get ramen and he reached out and held your hand on the crosswalk and he told you that you looked beautiful under the streetlights. When y'all were alone in your dorm watching a movie that played on your laptop that was settled on his legs and he asked you, quickly and quietly, if he could take you on a date and without looking at him, a sly smile spread across your lips, and told him yes. Before that, when your friends left to pick up late-night cookies and y'all were alone in his dorm and nothing happened, but everything happened, eyes locking for a long time and he grinned at you, looked away and that's when you knew. Before that, when y'all danced together until three a.m. and then sat on some stairs, drunk on adrenaline and shared each other's life stories. That night, a month into y'all's little yet vast relationship when you laid on the grass, next to him, and stared at the stars and talked about the meaning of life and he kissed you, meaningfully, passionately, and when he pulled away, his lips lingering on yours, he admitted to you that you were his first kiss. And when you asked him if he was happy about that, he said yes. Very happy.

You're not upset that you still remember everything, nor are you upset that you remember him. You hate to admit it, but you enjoy living in the past. You crave the hauntings, the feeling you get when you sink deep down into them. It can be more comforting than living in the present. And sometimes, you just can't forget people because really, you don't want to, you're always missing people, and so the stories continue to haunt you deep into the night, catch you in your sleep, creating allusions in your mind.

He was so real, more real than anything else. You felt him, all of him.

However, you never felt *it*. The spark to make things work, to meld things together, to turn lust into love. And neither did he. It was just a little spill, an allusion, a brief falsity against reality. A simple mix-up between what is real, and what is not.

You lie awake at night and wait for the haunting to begin. You know it'll arrive in time, either in your dreams or projected right in front of you. It's never quite the same, and yet, you prefer it that way.

Something Outside My Window

When I was a child, I saw something outside my window.

With a start, I awoke to the sound of movement, and my eyes darted to see something I've never quite forgotten. It stood there in the backyard, its arms outstretched to its sides, claws protruding beneath its furry hands, glinting beneath the full moon's bold light. It hunched its back, its head dipped down toward the earth, rising in quite an exaggerated manner each time it breathed. I sat up in bed, my covers spilling off me, as I stared at this beast. I was frozen stiff in motion, my heart caught in the base of my throat, and I couldn't breathe. Even at such a young age, I felt like I was trapped in time, and I knew I was in danger. Something about this raging beast, so close its snorts were audible, hot white in the cold air, made every inch of my skin crawl with fear.

That was when my palm slipped, and I fell back onto the bed, but not only that--my elbow banged against the wall, everything in my bedroom trembling and creating a ruckus. And the beast looked at me--I never took my eyes off him, holding my throbbing elbow with my opposite hand, turned on my side in bed. Its eyes were bright green and glowed against the night. There was no anger in its eyes, and in fact, the beast almost appeared human, in some peculiar way. Its eyes softened when they met my gaze, and it curled its massive, black paws into fists, shielding its claws.

There was more movement, and my eyes flickered to greet its location. Another beast appeared, this one smaller and more feminine. The larger beast gestured toward my window, and the smaller beast situated her gaze at me. Her rageful face softened, similarly to the larger beast's. But this beast, in some strange way, appeared loving, as though she was trying to tell me something meaningful using only her eyes.

They then exchanged a glance, one I was all too familiar with but wasn't sure how, then curled over into the figure of a large wolf and darted into the night without looking back. I watched them race on all fours, as though they had somewhere important to be, vanishing beyond the trees that lay just behind our backyard.

I once thought that perhaps, this occurrence was only a dream. I remember explaining the bizarre, but gut-wrenching experience to my parents and they only grinned at me, patted me on the head, and told me they'd have to cut down my sweets in the evenings. "It was only a nightmare," my mother had said, "I get them all of the time."

But of course, my mind returned to this dream throughout my upbringing. I'd bring it up around holidays, only to have it be dismissed by every older relative of mine. My mother's relatives, of course--we don't speak to my father's family for reasons unknown.

Sometimes, I'd awaken in the night to a rustling, a presence, but find nothing. No beast ever stood in my backyard again. To be honest, I thought I was going mad, forever haunted by a singular occurrence that arose during sleep.

As I grew older, however, I began to notice patterns. The noises only came at 12:01 am, just after midnight, and only during a full moon. I'd stay awake, eyeing the backyard like a hawk, or sometimes, if I was ever brave enough, I'd watch from the roof, crouching low, staying hidden. I'd always hear the rustling but never fully saw the beasts again. (At least, not until later, when it was too late.) I was never *quite* brave enough to search for them in the woods. But, I had a good feeling they were there. Sometimes, I could feel their eyes on me. In time, I was uncertain whether the past event was a dream, or not.

When I was a teenager, some of my neighbors had spotted bears in the Texas woods, lurking around from midnight to dawn, with powerful, green eyes and large claws. These claims were dismissed, though, when evidence never turned up.

Now, it makes sense. It was never a dream, nor noises manifested from possible insanity within. The sightings were never just stories. And my parents weren't what I thought they were.

I stand stiffly beside the police and paramedics as they clean the area, examining my parent's pale, swelled bodies, and ask me question after question after question. They had been shot in the night while on someone's property. Apparently, the owner thought they were bears, and claimed they weren't people at all. They swear it,

I look down at my parents, hand-in-hand, eyes both closed. They lie there, almost peacefully, despite their inevitable decay. I notice a tuft of black fur near my father's gunshot wound, a smear of blood at the corner of my mother's lips, and my gut twists with bereavement. Was everything I knew only a lie?

I share my childhood experience, or the dream, with the police. They don't understand what I'm trying to say, so I don't push it. Especially when they begin to eye me, quite curiously with a subtle hint of concern lining their brows.

When I return home later that afternoon, dumbfounded as is, unable to collect my racing thoughts and frazzled emotions, the rest of my mother's family is already there, waiting for me by the fire. My grandfather withdraws a cigar from his lips, puffing out clouds of white smoke and smiling at me. I cannot tell if it is a genuine smile, or one of possession. A crazed man admiring his materialistic collections, perhaps even well-cared-for vehicles.

"It's about time you knew who you were, in blood and flesh," my grandfather begins. I press my shoulder to the wall, imagining that I am only a painting, and vanish entirely. This cannot possibly be happening. "Your transition will begin tonight."

"Don't worry," my aunt chimes in, smirking devilishly, when she notices the way I try to hide myself. "It only hurts a little."

It Wasn't Me

There had been many theories about how she had been murdered. Some people speculated that it was me, that I killed her. But oh, how untrue such a proposition was. How could have I murdered her? I had an alibi--I wasn't *there*. And I loved her, with all my heart. How could I have murdered someone I couldn't envision my life without? That just wouldn't make sense. Not in the slightest.

We had gotten in a fight earlier in the night, sure. Couples fight, that's just what they do. Some call it anger, I call it passion. She had been texting her ex, but big deal--I text my ex, too. She didn't need to know this, though. I suppose the fight was fueled by projection, in a way. At least, that's what a psychologist would say. I'm no psychologist. My mom is. She's tried diagnosing me herself, but I never listened. Isn't that against some sort of underlining code, anyway? Who would let their own mother diagnose them? Not me. I'm fine. In fact, I find that I'm more mentally capable than most of these idiots in the world. Most people let their emotions get to them, let their feelings knock them down and hold them there. They get… *empathetic* toward people they don't even know, try to make changes from across the globe via Reddit like they're some kind of hero, waste their time helping their toxic friends through their 4th breakup of the month. Life is too short to feel bad for strangers, or for people clearly far below ourselves.

Anyway, I'm getting off track. We had gotten in a fight, as couples do, and I left. Simple as that. I joined my friend at our favorite local pub, ordered a dark ale, then walked home in the dark. Have you ever walked alone at night? It's incredibly soothing. And quiet. The fireflies glitter along the road and the streetlamps hum and flicker and spill white illuminance into the darkness. I do a lot of thinking when I walk at night, and I still do. Especially after an ale, the warmth of it settling in my chest like fuzz and making my eyes go dewy, my mind relaxed. I think too much, I do, and sometimes I need those night walks, the air crisp and cold on my bare skin, the breeze wisping through my hair, to let the thoughts, oftentimes thoughts no one should ever hear, secrets kept only for myself, slip out into the empty blackness of the suburban streets and shrink into nothingness against the shadows.

When I got home, she was dead. Gruesomely so, naked on the floor, her throat slit open, blood soaking our cream-colored carpet. I barely had time to react emotionally, calling the police the moment I saw, and they rushed over right away. I never cried, which is when the speculation started, but sometimes people don't cry. They can't. Paralyzed with fear of the unknown, they don't know how they can move on. They can't possibly move on, and the very thought of doing so is excruciating. I sat in the corner of the living room after they moved her body and marked the crime scene and asked me all the questions. They asked me to stand, to step outside for some fresh air, but I couldn't. I just couldn't. My eyes were two spheres of glass, unmoving, unblinking, my muscles still and my mind somewhere beyond previous limitations. My thoughts were not my own and my brain could not control my body and hell, I dissociated right there on the floor and saw myself beyond my body and they *still* thought I did it. It's always the husband, they had said through their cracked red lipstick in the corner of the wake while drinking stale champagne because her father was a cheapskate. What selfish bastards they were, every one of her stupid friends and family members. She was too good for them, always had been. She was too good for me, even, but she never thought so herself. For a long time, I didn't know what to do with myself, without her. She made me a better man, prevented me from slipping back into old ways.

Since then, I've moved on. Physically and mentally. For a while I was a suspect, but without any evidence, they let me go, and I moved down by the beach, away from the chaos and the allegations and the sole memory of the woman I loved. It was too painful to even be present in the same city, every restaurant, coffee shop, every goddamn corner reminding me of her and what could have been.

My buddy told the police that I had been there with him, that I wasn't at the house, that I couldn't have *possibly* done it. Even the bar manager and a handful of customers confirmed that I was there, sitting on one of those uncomfortably small wooden barstools, gulping down my ale like chilled water on a hot, summer day. I wasn't *there*. I just wasn't.

Some people assumed that I had killed her *before* the pub and left her there, slit her throat mid-fight and left her cold carcass lying on the floor, went to go drink my sorrows away before deciding to call the cops, giving them false times when I did, before putting on my show. They assumed that I didn't *want* to kill her, and that I wasn't even completely sure of what I had done, and many people assumed I wasn't well--a sociopath, they like to say--and did it swiftly, without really thinking about doing it, just wanting to *feel* something, but realizing that I was entirely incapable of ever feeling anything at all, and while I was sad for her death, as sad as I could possibly be, it wasn't entirely my fault. And not being able to cry, that wasn't my fault either. I was scared. I didn't want her to leave me. I couldn't phantom the idea of being alone. If I hadn't done it, she would've left me, in time, and I couldn't let that happen. I loved her, I did. I just got so angry. So… *mad*. So frantic. And I just did it. I grabbed her by the hair and I grabbed the knife and before I could even stop myself, before I could even pause long enough to look her in the eyes and realize it was her, my wife, my best friend, she was gone.

But, of course, that is all just a theory. A simple speculation. People, and their profound admiration for rumors… oh, how it humors me.

She Was There, And Then She Wasn't

My heart continued to ache powerfully three months after the breakup. It was as though Ashley left just the day before, the ache a fresh wound that stung constantly and bled worse at night when I was truly alone. My body had weakened, every movement sluggish like I was trudging through thick mud. Nothing made sense anymore, including my life. The more my mother protested that I'd heal with time, the more I began distrusting her advice. In fact, it seemed to worsen as time went on. I kept reminding myself that Ashley had chased after Tyler the day after our split--she was *fine* without me. But this thought only worsened the sting. She had somebody, and I didn't. I strolled through the days alone, my head fogged with heavy clouds, seeing only the top of her blonde hair beyond the crowds during passing periods. Every glimpse of her, every brief thought, even, panged like hell. Ashley was my first kiss, first time, first *girlfriend*, after all. I wasn't sure how to go on without her near me. It was like a hole had been punctured in my chest and as the wind howled through, I was blown back again and again.

At least Sophie was there. She and I had been acquaintances all semester, and I hadn't thought much of her until a month after my breakup. She was pretty, without a doubt, with soft features and a bright smile, but she was quiet. One day, out of my desperate need to fill the expanding emptiness that continued to swell, I slipped her my number. Her eyes had flickered to mine briefly before she turned away completely, her cheeks rosy, her teeth gnawing on her bottom lip. I had never seen her grin so hard before. Later that evening, she called me, her voice soft but jittery, and that's how it started.

    For our first date, we went to a local burger joint, which I had suggested. It wasn't anything memorable, but I had a nice time. Sophie showed up with curled hair and pink lip gloss, revealing a figure I didn't know she had. She didn't speak much, mostly just listened as I unintentionally spilled my life onto her. She nodded to everything I said, even frowned and murmured responses when she was supposed to. When I asked about her, she fell quiet and always turned the conversation back to me, seemingly mesmerized by my family issues and stress regarding college applications and SAT scores.

    After dinner, we strolled to the ice cream parlor next door. She ordered raspberry truffle, I ordered vanilla, and we sat ourselves down on a metal bench outside, a little too close, with our cones in hand. Sitting next to her, I felt as though I had always belonged at her side. We fell into a natural rhythm of asking each other existential questions while tracing the constellations with our eyes. She briefly mentioned that she wanted to be a writer but wasn't sure if she'd ever write anything worth reading, and to this day, I still wish I had asked her why that was.

    Later that evening, I sobbed Ashley's name into my pillow.

Sophie and I went on a few more dates after that. Once to the park, where we shared a long and meaningful kiss beneath the stars. I held her against my chest, our bodies molding together like puzzle pieces that fit just right, except for her elbow that dug a little too much into my side. That night, she told me that she could sense a darkness within me sometimes and wished she could take it from me so I wouldn't have to carry so much weight. When I asked her how often she sensed the darkness, she replied, "Only when the excitement has worn off and there's nothing left to distract you."

"That's deep," I said before pecking her on the lips.

We also went to the movies once, where we sat in the back of the theatre and made out most of the time. We left with shy smiles and crazed hair, giggling all the way to that same ice cream parlor. She ordered coffee nut, I ordered vanilla.

I mostly just saw Sophie in school. I'd accompany her to the buses after our class together, where we'd pass notes and occasionally hold hands. At the bus stop, I'd give her a sweet hug goodbye before walking to the parking lot, and scanning the crowd for Ashley's face, just for a moment. Sometimes I'd see her, laughing alongside Tyler or a handful of girlfriends, and a thick cloud of despair would overcome me and follow me all the way home, settling in the corners of my room, watching me.

Sophie and I'd call late into the night, and while she didn't talk much, I always felt giddy in preparation for those calls. I'd share my day, and she'd skim over hers, and we'd talk about everything and anything under the sun. Or at least, she'd ask the questions, and I'd give the responses. We had come to discover that we had much in common, and just enough not in common so that the conversation remained interesting. She loved Star Wars with a passion, and so did I. She loved reading, which I didn't enjoy as much, preferring movies instead, but we both had the same favorite genre: Adventure. We were both only children. We both had one living parent.

Even with her soft nature, the conversations were always interesting; she always knew exactly how to respond. With Sophie, that dull ache in my chest, the sting of the wound, would escape my consciousness, becoming forgotten for a fleeting moment. However, with the absence of Sophie's voice, the pain would spring back up and haunt me deep into dawn. The pain wasn't as prominent as before, now that I had someone, but it still remained. Some nights were worse than others, and I wasn't sure if I'd be able to survive. I'd clutch at my heart and glower at the despair and expanding emptiness that continued hovering in the corner, mocking me now. I'd sob to melancholy music, praying that the helplessness would finally leave. While I cried, Sophie would text me, "I had fun on the phone! Goodnight :)"

I knew things with Sophie wouldn't last forever, but her presence made me feel warm and full, each day that pit of my stomach shrinking just a bit. Although the nights alone trekked on forever, and memories of Ashley and I would welcome me in my sleep, awaking me with a painful start, I was beginning to feel confident in myself and in my growth. It had been five months, after all, and I could finally see glimmers of light protruding from the other side. I could rise out of bed without a weakness holding me down. I *could* get over Ashley. I wasn't sure when I would, but I knew that patience was in my favor.

That is until one evening at 3 a.m I received a text message: *Tyler was a mistake. I miss you.*

I could've sworn that my deep-rooted passion for Ashley had dissipated by then, but I was far from right. The moment I received this text, the flame erupted within and I sprung out of bed with a wild smile on my face. With trembling hands, I responded: *Hey you. How's it been?*

The worst part was that I didn't tell Sophie. Abruptly, I had stopped responding to her texts, told her I was too busy with college applications to call. However, I did continue walking her to the buses and continued holding her hand during class. She'd smile at me, ask me how I was doing, all the while I was just hoping things would fizzle out soon. Or, when summer break hit that next week, I could permanently ignore her. And Sophie never questioned my sudden distance, and I knew she never would, considering her quietness. She would understand when I left completely, just as she understood most things.

I had never felt so whole, so full, being back together with Ashley. I only met with her outside of school, in hopes Sophie wouldn't see us together or Ashley wouldn't see me holding Sophie's hand in the hallways, but it wasn't that much of a hassle. Besides this, everything seemed to be working out for me. I'd give

Ashley a ride home with the windows down, and sometimes we'd stop for ice cream. She'd order strawberry, and so would I. After listening to her rant about her volleyball team drama, or whatever else had occurred that day to infuriate her, we'd head back to my house and snuggle up in the media room until dinner time. My previous pain was long forgotten and had been replaced with a bright passion within. Life seemed exciting now, not just bearable.

  On the last day of school, Sophie ignored me for the entirety of class, not even glancing my way. When the final bells rang and everyone cheered for summer break, she left in a hurry without a hint as to why. My stomach briefly twisted as I watched her round the corner and walk away, her absence leaving me feeling hollow. Silence hung in the air like poison, despite the thrilled cheers erupting from the hallways.

  I stayed in the room a while longer, staring at my hands, my breath caught in my throat. That's when my teacher said to me, "You messed up, huh? Better fix it fast." My eyes lifted to meet him as he gestured toward Sophie's seat. Then, he smiled. "Have a great summer, son." He left, leaving me all alone, and completely still.

  It was that moment when I realized a small part of me did care for Sophie, and I began to wonder how she was doing since our last call. Did she ever get into NYU? Did she begin writing anything worth reading? These questions sat in the back of my throat and left a bad taste in my mouth. I knew it was far too late to ask them.

Eventually, I gathered my things and met with Ashley in the parking lot, and we went back to my place, just as we always did. And although I seemingly had everything I ever wanted, there was a small piece of myself still missing.

That same night, I received a text from Sophie: *I understand now. You're back with her. How foolish of me, to think that we had something meaningful. Thank you for your time, and have a nice summer.*

And six hours later, I replied: *I'm sorry.*

A heaviness weighed on me throughout the next few days, then lifted, and while I occasionally thought of Sophie, I never reached out again. At least, not until a few months into college. I had a marvelous summer with Ashley, spending days at the beach and an entire weekend at a neighboring hotel. Then, she broke up with me in September and got back with Tyler. For some reason, the second breakup wasn't as painful. Yet, the darkness, the heaviness that comes after all heartbreak, returned for a few weeks, making time move slowly and grand dreams meaningless.

When I was at my lowest, I reached out to Sophie: *Hey. I'm sorry again for everything. Do you want to meet up for coffee sometime?*

The moment I sent the text, I remembered she was in New York, and I was still in Colorado. But, that didn't matter anyway--she never responded. It was as if she was there, and then she… wasn't.

Winter break, I returned home, alone, but okay. On a crisp Tuesday, my mother and I visited the local grocery store when I saw her, Sophie, her fingers entwined with another man's, who I couldn't quite see from where I stood and still have no idea who he could've possibly been. Her head was tilted back, giggling at something he had said, and her eyes crinkled with joy, pure joy. I had never seen her laugh so hard until that moment, had never seen so much light radiating off of her like natural illuminance. She was more than pretty. She was beautiful. She was… everything I could've ever wanted, and I let her slip between my fingers like the wind.

    They rounded the corner together, and they were gone.

She Looked at Me

I looked at her, looked at the way her deep brown hair draped over her shoulders and covered most of her face, looked at the way her sapphire eyes peered at me from beneath the loose strands. She tilted her head and pursed her lips, and her eyes, wide and curious, glanced me up and down. She was wearing a white dress and that was all, really--she had no shoes or accessories. It was just her and that blindingly white dress. It was so white, it made me mad. I wanted it to go away.

Her eyes met mine again, and she smiled. It wasn't a nice smile, however, nor was it in any way inviting. It was evil and menace and had a slight curl to it that made my entire body shiver. It became strangely cold in the room, with her here.

She scrunched her nose, as though she smelled something foul, and I counted six freckles along her cheeks. She furrowed her eyebrows, too, and her eyes trailed my face. The smile was now gone and was replaced with a deep frown that dug deep into her face. Why she was frowning, I don't know.

She itched her ear, and mine felt itchy as well, but I didn't dare lift my hand--I left it dangling at my side because she had no power over me anymore. Not anymore. I was my own being, far different from whatever she was. She didn't believe me and laughed a dark, ugly laugh that shook the room. But, I only stared. I did not laugh. I didn't even try.

"Susan?" the nurse called from behind me.

I looked over my shoulder at him and said nothing. His face was hard, like a rock, his jaw razor sharp. His eyes were small and dark, two buttons sewn onto a doll.

"It's time for dinner, Susan," the nurse said, smiling, motioning me toward him.

A grin trembled onto my lips, and although I hesitated, I stepped away from the mirror, tiptoeing out of the room, hoping that she couldn't hear me leaving. I knew, however, that I'd have to face her when I returned.

Versions of Myself

I.

      Pressed against the wall in a crowded room. Clinging to the only person I know like a life raft. A soft smile stiff on my lips, my face as unmoving as stone. My chest feels tight, my breath constrained as the thick body heat and blaring music fills the crevices of my mind and traps me, holds me down. I imagine being in my bedroom, reading a good novel, drinking a warm cup of tea, and I ease. But only a little. I'm introduced to someone new, and I'm so cheery, my voice elevating in pitch and cracking along the edges as I say my name and ask them theirs and then we're talking about something simple and surface level until the conversation slowly diminishes and my beam fades back into a tight grin. Kind, sweet, nice. That's what I am, now. There are no lights besides a few dazzling bulbs strung overhead, blanketing the space in a warm illuminance. The music vibrates beneath my shoes, traveling through the wood flooring, and I feel it. I observe the people from a distance, chatting among themselves, and briefly, I wonder why I can't be more normal. Eventually, I make my way into the crowds, toward a circle I vaguely recognize, apologizing to the few people who accidentally bump into me, but I don't say much. No, I mostly just admire, perceive. The truth is, I'm terrified. Terrified that no one will talk to me, that no one actually wants me in this circle right now. So, I simply watch, an observer, noticing fashion choices, angles of faces, body language, everyone's different figures, picking up on any underlying social cues, such as noticing someone feeling uncomfortable about something someone else said, or someone else eager for attention, for the spotlight, or someone else completely tuned out and restless to leave the conversation, but is unsure how to do so. It's like this game I play, reading people. Seeing through their masks. Picking apart their secrets that have begun to leak out over the course of the night, thanks to the hard liquor and fatigue that has begun to set in. My friend tells everyone that I'm an author, and I blush, turn away, and when they tell me how awesome such an accomplishment is, I shrug and tell them that writing is just a hobby of mine, it's nothing special. Occasionally, I'll try to speak up, prepare something wise and interesting to say, but rarely do the words bound from my lips, and when they do, they sometimes fall flat, resulting in an uncomfortable lapse of silence. However, other times they *do* make people laugh. That makes me feel good. But I'm constantly worried, I think, about whether people like me. Worried about saying the wrong thing, not saying enough. Worried that the moment I leave the conversation, the gossiping will start. Perhaps this is why I don't say much; sometimes, the less you say, the less people have to say negatively about you. Right? Someone turns to me, asks me about my book. Someone else mentions that I have a grounded presence about me. Comments like these are the sort of validation I need tonight. Notice how I said need.

II.

Sprawled out along my bed on a cold, rainy day, the gray sky shifting beyond my window, clouds traversing the world at a steady pace. I feel so safe, so cozy, so at peace with myself. I'm staring up at the ceiling, listening to a playlist made up of melancholy and euphoric music that always makes me feel deep and important when I listen to it. Special. Unique. I'm so edgy, aren't I? I'm thinking of life and how odd it is. How we are really just sacks of organs. How the ocean isn't really blue but carries the illusion that it is. How we keep little animals inside of our homes just because we want to, because they snuggle up with us and give us a sense of purpose. How funny it is that we put so much emphasis on how we look when we're all going to grow old one day. How in a several hundred years, the only reminder of me will be my relatives, or perhaps even my stories, hopefully. How in a several hundred years, the Earth might not even be here, who knows. How fascinatingly strange our brains are. How we see images in our mind, hear voices in our head, watch thoughts trail by, and how odd that is. How no one will ever know how we truly feel, and how we will never know how others truly feel, about us, about other things. How everyone we know, including us, will someday die. How everyone probably thinks about things like this but will never actually say them out loud, and I'm always curious as to why that is. It's probably because if we did, we'd be seen as weird. Odd. Socially awkward. When we share opinions, we might offend someone. When we share accomplishments, we might come across as conceited.

When we share our pain, we are being a downer. When we are happy, we are fake. When we are sad, we are depressing. When we work on ourselves, on our bodies, we don't like ourselves. When we sit around all day, we don't like ourselves, either. I think about how, in the end, it really doesn't matter how we choose to live our lives, because this life doesn't belong to anyone but ourselves. We decide the course of our brief, momentary lives from here. I think about how strange it is, that we are on a floating rock in space and yet, we give things so much meaning. The world revolves around ourselves despite the fact that we are small. So, very small. I like it here, deep down in my thoughts, submerged in this ocean. Strange things happen down here, but it's also where I find my ideas. I feel comforted, here in my mind.

III.

Headphones in. Music on, usually Pitbull or Lady Gaga or anything fast that I hate to admit I actually enjoy listening to. I reach down, touch my fingers to the earth, stretching my hamstrings, my glutes. I breathe in deeply, think of something positive, breathe out deeply. I got this. I rise up, pull my arms across my chest, one after the other. Lift my knee, hug it against myself. Then the other. I am ready. I start my workout on my Apple Watch, and then I'm going, jogging into the street, swaying my arms back and forth, my lips slightly parted as I breathe, easily, lightly. This is one of my favorite times of the day, the air fresh and dewy and the breeze cool on my skin. My left tennis shoe lands in a puddle, splashes me a little. My chest starts to tighten now, and so do my calves, as I near a half mile. It goes by so quickly because I get so lost in my thoughts. What do I need to pick up at the grocery store today? I should really ask her to hang out. Are my pieces actually good enough to be published? I catch myself in the act, force myself to smile. I got this. I am strong. I'm at a mile when I start to really get tired. My breath is hot and heavy and sweat beads on my upper lip, which I dab away with my tank top. My chest tightens, my stomach knotted, strands of my hair sticking to my wet cheeks. The trees are so pretty, so tall overhead, like mighty giants, their green leaves swaying. I admire them from down here, trying to distract my raging thoughts, the swelling aches. Come on, keep going. I feel myself start to slow, my mind now arguing with my body, encouraging and tempting my feet to suddenly just, stop. But I don't. I got this. I pay attention to the music again, the rhythm thudding throughout me, carrying my achy feet forward. I disappear into the beats, a comforting home inside my head, and imagine that I'm in a movie, running from zombies or aliens or just running because I'm cool. I am strong. So, very strong. One more mile, I tell myself at two. That's always the hardest one, the third. But I'm so close. I'm almost done. I'm basically hopping at this point, no longer jogging. Anyone who sees me might think I've been running for hours, but it's been only twenty minutes. I love it, this feeling. I couldn't tell you why. This achy sensation, pushing my body to its limit, feeling my strength, my power, feeling myself push past the doubt, past the limited beliefs, my breath now raspy and my face searing with heat. When I've reached three miles, I stop rather abruptly and then I walk around for a while, sipping the dense air like water. I smile. Maybe even laugh. I did it. Yes, I did it.

IV.

    I'm at a coffee shop with a wonderful conversationalist or someone I'm fairly close with or maybe even very close with and I'm talking a mile a minute. About the book I'm working on, about the three books I'm reading, about any troubles in my life, about my deepest fears and insecurities, about stones and their spiritual abilities, about my profound love of yoga, about what I'm currently working on at my job, about the classes I'm taking this semester, about where I want to live in the future, what I want my house to look like, about how Tots, my cat, is doing, about some psychological theory I just learned about, about my favorite antique shop downtown, about my relationship and how it's going, about all the things I have to get done that day, about this brilliant movie I watched the other day about the making of a sociopath, about anything and everything under the sun and perhaps even beyond the sun. I'll talk about deep space, if you'd like. If you ask me questions, I will answer them. If you help carry the conversation, prove to me that you're trustworthy, that you won't judge, it won't take me long to open up, to lift my wall. This can end up being dangerous in the future, but right now it's okay. I crack wide open to you and share everything, all of my thoughts, and you drink me up, me and all of my thoughts. My feelings. My secrets. My laugh carries itself through the space, my smile genuine, big and bold on my face. You talk, too, about your life, things you enjoy, what you have going on that day. I love listening, to stories, to projects, to goals, to things you love, to what troubles you. I take a long sip of my latte, frothy with a hint of cinnamon, and I focus on you and the words you say. Come to me, and I will listen, I will help. I love to help. I love to socialize, but only when it's just me, and you, and no one else. You're surprised--usually I'm so quiet in groups, you tell me. Yes, I agree, and I don't really know why. And I'll talk about that, too, bring up some psychology concept that might explain why I am the way I am because there always has to be something special regarding the decisions I make. I am an open book, I just am, when I feel safe. When I feel seen. Am I sharing too much to you now? Probably, but that's okay. I feel safe here, with you. Ohmigosh, we have to hang out more often.

V.

Enya humming softly in the background. A glass of chardonnay on my desk, a candle flickering light on my walls, the sun setting, night creeping up from below and darkening my bedroom, creating a comforting space. My fingers trail the keyboard, and I am immersed in the screen. In the story. It's like my consciousness disappears. An idea will strike, a beaming lightbulb in my mind, and it won't leave until I write it down. Just like this piece, this very one. It takes me an hour, sometimes even less, to write a piece like this. I'm not sure why I do it so fast, so easily. I always have, ever since I was little. The words just pour out of me like a running faucet, decorating themselves along the page. It's like my fingers already know what to do, writing randomness, but randomness that usually always has a deeper meaning and makes some sort of sense to me. Flowery, that's how people describe my writing. Brave. Different. Unafraid to try new things. Perhaps that is only them being kind. I like to describe writing as painting an abstract work of art, how all you really have to do is release all expectations and splatter on some red. Streak on some green. Smother in some blue. Whatever your mind calls you to do, whatever you feel like adding, lean into that. Have fun with it, writing. It's been a long time since I've written like this, almost every day. Sitting down to write a piece that's been bulging in my mind, stubborn, not letting go. And when I'm done writing, a wave of relief washes over me, and I return to equilibrium. Maybe that's why my pieces always come across as "dark"--writing is how I heal. Understand. Release. I grin like a fool, tears brimming my eyes, as I read what I've written over and over again. Maybe it's a bit arrogant, to be this proud of my work. But that's what I am. Proud. Proud of how far I've come. Proud of where I might go. Proud of my ability to turn a blank page into something meaningful. At least, to me. I dream of the possibilities, of where my craft will take me. It doesn't hurt to dream. I've held onto this dream since I was a child, writing in my well-used journal at the kitchen table, at recess, outside under the summer sun. Who knows when I'll get there, if I'll get there. In the meantime, I'll keep writing. I'll keep chasing those lightbulbs, those urges. I'll disappear into the worlds, the stories, the unfiltered trains of thought. I'll lose myself in the words, in the feel of my fingertips, now rubbed raw and sore, as they dance, wildly, on the keys, all throughout the night, well past my bedtime, when my brain is all but mush, the warmth from the chardonnay settling in my chest, and there is nothing left inside of me except peace. I have many versions of myself, I'm well aware. But I feel most like myself when I'm writing, alone. When it is finally dark outside, the moon bold in the black sky, and all is quiet, as I read my finished piece. Look at you, Brittney. I breathe in a shaky breath; I always get emotional when I read my thoughts after they've settled on the page, finally visible to me. My thoughts can be difficult to figure out, I think, scrambled up in my mind, but when I write them down, that's when all is clear. That's when I truly look at myself, truly see myself, vulnerable and raw and unafraid and whole. Staring at my writing, at the mirror, which reflects back a face, a mind that I haven't acknowledged in quite some time, due to the fact that it's been stuffed deep down beneath all of the other versions of myself. There is no true version of myself, but this one, it feels the most right.

Alone, Together

Walking toward the bus stop on a rainy Tuesday afternoon, just after work, she glanced into a cafe where she saw a table occupied by four women, roughly her age, sipping their frothy lattes and giggling over something one of them had said. The sight left her feeling hollow and deeply, she sighed. Continued walking. In an alleyway, she spotted a young couple, hand-in-hand, dressed up rather nicely for a Tuesday, wild beams on their faces. Once again, she sighed, her chest weighed down with a feeling of… hopelessness. She didn't want to feel this way. No, not at all. But she had been alone for so long now. Too long.

She arrived at the bus stop, wrapped her arms around herself, pulling her bright, red coat closer, and stared at the young man opposite of her. A book was opened and held between his palms, and his face, a black beard neatly trimmed around thin lips, was dipped toward it. He appeared deeply engrossed by the book. She, a reader, tried to see what the book was, but couldn't see the cover from where she stood. She wanted to ask, but didn't want to disturb him, so she turned away, focused on the rain that had just begun to drizzle. Her breath was white in the air, and she shuddered, but she rather enjoyed the cold. Crisp on her skin, like little teeth, biting.

Her gaze returned to the man. Like his beard, his hair was black and crazed, but in a handsome sort of way.

He was very handsome, from what she could see of him. He looked about her age, too. From what she could see. She wondered what he did for a living, wondered if he had any plans that evening. She didn't have any plans, but that was normal. Truthfully, she was a homebody. At the end of the day, she enjoyed her stash of ordain cheeses, the cabernet sauvignon that made her lips pucker, then melt into a grin, her candles, her quiet. She did, truly. In all honesty, the idea of friends, a clingy relationship, sounded rather annoying. But then again, she didn't want to be alone *all* of the time. No, not all of the time.

    The handsome man glanced up, looked at her, and although she wanted to smile, she ended up twisting her gaze away from him. Why, she didn't know. Perhaps nerves? It had been an awfully long time since she had done this, spoken to an attractive man with hopes of getting to know him. Or, eye-flirt, more like. But, did she truly want to get to know him? Was this even an intelligent idea? No, probably not. But her chest, it swelled with butterflies that rose up to the base of her throat, and her fingertips settled there, feeling her heartbeat race beneath her skin.

    She waited for him to say something to her. He should be the one to speak first, right? He was the man, after all, and she the woman. So he should be the one to make the first move. And she knew he would--she could feel his eyes on her, staring, admiring her and her confidence, she hoped. Her independence. Her beauty, perhaps? There was a lingering feeling that passed between them, almost as though it pulled them closer together, this bus stop their own, this moment belonging to them, only.

Her eyes lifted, glanced at him. He had returned to his book, nose-deep. She imagined what their conversation would be like, when he spoke to her. Which he would. It went something like this:

"Hello, there. I love that red coat you're wearing." His voice would be deep, dark. Chocolatey. Sweetly rich to the ears.

"Thank you," she'd say, blushing. "I rather like the color red. What book are you reading?"

"Oh, I'm reading this contemporary novel about a couple who love each other but fail to communicate their feelings and their relationship results in a breakup, but they reunite many years later only to discover they had mutual feelings all along."

"Wow, you seem intellectual."

He'd chuckle. "I like to think so."

"I also like to read."

"Yeah? What kinds of books?"

"Primarily thrillers, or mysteries. Sometimes horror, if I'm feeling up to it."

"Oh! I love horror, but only when I'm not alone."

She'd dip her chin. "Unfortunately, I'm always alone." She'd glance back up, soften her eyes. "I'm sorry, that came off rather melancholy."

He'd close his book, lower it to his side, and his expression would loosen, become more inviting. "No, not at all. In fact, I am lonely myself."

"Is that so? How come?"

"I have no one to share this life with. It is only me, and my books."

"But is that such a bad thing?"

He'd shake his head, then sigh. "I'm not sure. I'd like to experience life with someone, I suppose. I'd like to share the stories I read, the adventures I go on. At least, a friend. Someone to talk to."

"Me, too," she'd reply. "That would be nice."

A brief lapse of silence would pass, then he would turn to her and say, "Well, in that case, perhaps I could take you out to dinner?"

"Me? Really?" She'd beam, revealing her left dimple, her cheeks rosy red.

"I mean, why not? You're a beautiful woman, and in need of company I presume. Just like me."

"Why, I would love to be taken out to dinner by you."

"Are you free tonight?"

Her eyes would widen. "Tonight? But, it's Tuesday, and it's rainy, and--" She'd cut herself off, staring into his eyes and sighing a breath of release. She had never done something of this sort before. In fact, it could be dangerous. It most certainly was. And yet, all her dreams had seemed to come true, flourishing right in front of her. For the first time in ages, she was no longer alone. At least, not alone in her feelings of loneliness. "Yes. Absolutely, I am free tonight."

"Wonderful. Then, it's a date."

He blinked when the bus arrived, and he fell out of his trance. He closed his book, which he wasn't *really* reading, and stuffed it under his armpit, glancing at her one last time. Her eyes, so beautiful, so brown, stared back at him. It was almost as though she was calling to him, waiting for him to say something. He watched her part her lips, then hesitate. He waited for her to say something. When she didn't, pressing her lips back into a line, he sighed, climbed the bus and settled into the back. He stared at the beautiful woman from the window, spotted with rain, and wished he had spoken to her. Why didn't he speak to her? Nerves, perhaps?

    The bus rolled away toward his home, where he would have a quiet evening alone, with his book.

Is This Life Not Already Enough?

We are sinful sinners.

My toes curl into the soft, moist grass and I feel the earth hum beneath my feet, vibrating with warm life. A gentle breeze wisps past me, strands of my hair rising with it to stroke my cheeks, getting caught between my dry lips. My eyes close and I feel the crisp air on my skin, hear the birds chirping within the trees, their songs being carried throughout the forest. The scent of fresh plantation, blossoming life, and dew overwhelms my senses. I inhale deeply, feeling all of this goodness flood my lungs with an airy lightness, and I exhale everything, my fears, my pain, my uncertainties, and Nature takes it as it is, takes me as I am, and She welcomes me in, and I, like the birds and the air and the trees, am a part of everything.

There is only one true way to live. Only one true belief. Only one correct way of thinking.

I love to learn. I always have. Ways of life, tales of history, I am engrossed by it all, intrigued by the lives lived before mine, in the lives lived across the Universe and through time. Humanity, and the stories we tell, and the battles we've fought, and the progress we've made, and our faults, our defeats. This is why I read so many books, I suppose. I cannot get enough of them. Stories. My fingers are frantic, turning each page, absorbing each word, listening to these stories and taking them on as my own. Life is too short to live only a single life. To not have an open mind. To not wonder, to not question.

God is our one true love. Trust in him. Have grace.

    I reach out toward him, drift my fingertips over his soft skin, and he stirs softly. I stroke his hair, always crazed, always velvety smooth to the touch, and entwine a strand in my fingers. He's so peaceful, lying here beside me, so beautiful to me, in all of his flaws, all of his imperfections. They're perfect, to me, because he is human, because he is him, truly and entirely.

    My head lies on his chest, warm, and I rise and fall with his every breath. We are connected, alive. There is no one I'd rather spend this brief life with. He is my true love. *Your true life begins once you meet Him. This temporary life is merely a test.*

    My chest swells with a deep, thunderous pain, and fades to nothingness. This is when I cry.

    My heart thuds wildly as I run, splitting the air as I do, feeling the hard ground beneath my feet, the wind on my bare skin, the sticky sweat on my cheeks.

    My eyes widen and the corners of my lips twist upwards into a beam. And I'm laughing, uncontrollably, hoping that this moment, this ache in my gut, this unconditional love, will never end.

    I'm alone, writing this story, or whatever it is, my fingers trembling as I do, confused as to why I'm writing it at all, but knowing, deep down that this is what I want to do. It is what I need to do.

    I'm still in the forest, and now I am at a pond, staring down at my reflection, who stares back up and smiles at me, a look of recognition crossing her eyes. Kneeling beside the pond, my gaze lifts to meet the sky, the sun brilliant and shining a puddle of warmth over me, it's light glinting off the swaying trees. Carefully, I part my lips to speak, and I ask, to whomever is listening,

> *Is this life not already enough?*
> *Am I, exactly as I am, not already enough?*

Part 3
Forwards, Straight Up

This Is What Strength Looks Like

I like to admire my muscles sometimes. Is that odd? Especially during yoga, when I'm in tabletop position, inhaling to cat, exhaling to cow, and I notice my biceps protruding, my arms shadowed against the trickle of light that flutters in from my window. I lift my hand to the ceiling, twisting my body, "massaging my organs", and I notice the pocket of my shoulder, the flex of the muscle there, a rounded bump on the top of my arm. Even my hands and wrists are different now, dainty and yet, powerful, like they could hold anything, do anything.

I've never had muscles like this before, ever. Not even while I was a full-time swimmer back in the day. Perhaps it's age, an increase in protein, lifting heavier weights… whatever the case, I have muscle now. It's foreign to me, doesn't feel like it should be there, doesn't feel like I'm worthy to have it. It was never my goal to have muscle, to be strong. It never even crossed my mind those months ago when I began. I didn't think I wanted it, all this power, all this strength.

But now I'm obsessed with it. I'm infatuated with the new curvatures of my body, the swell of my arms and legs after a completed workout, the aches that follow into the next day. I'm not for sure why, especially because I've never been one to admire strength. I prefer solitude, daintiness, cozy candlelight flickering against the darkness I'm encased in, bleeding onto the page and creating worlds and imaginations against the white canvas. Not…

intensity, lifting heavy, pre-workout drinks, whey protein, 10,000 steps a day. No, these things have never been likes of mine. And yet now, they're all I can think about. The progress, the speed, the way old clothes now fit on my frame, the peak of muscles from beneath the several layers of skin.

Yet, it extends beyond that. It's the way I feel, mentally. Like I can accomplish anything.

I grab my arm when I'm nervous and feel my tricep muscle, tight like a rock on my arm and I almost pause, thinking, "This isn't my arm. No, it can't be." But it is. And I think to myself, "This is what strength looks like."

Sometimes at night, when I'm alone, I cry about nothing. Well, not nothing, usually something. But, a something so insignificant, it really is nothing. And I withhold the tears to the best of my ability, but eventually, they seep out, and the emotions pool around me, fill my lungs and drown me. In time, I stop, and I rise, and I fetch a book to read.

Other times, I simply stare. At nothing, at something, sometimes with my eyes closed. Whatever the case, my eyes harden at whatever lies before me and my thoughts, they slip out from the grasp in my mind and are released into the world, and I let them. I don't reach out to grab them. No, not anymore. I have learned, I think, when it is time to let go.

The past comes to me, homing in the crevices of my mind, my blind spots, emerging when I least expect it, when I least want it. I once allowed the memories, the guilt, the pain, to swell, but it's funny because now, I've come to realize that the past no longer exists. No, it is no longer here. "You're not real," I say to it, and I watch it tremble and shrink to nothing. All that's left are the few shards, composed of lessons to learn and moments that serve some importance, some value. I live in my skin, presently, living now, no longer housing in this home in my head. At least, not nearly as often.

    My skin, it peels, after having been licked by the sun, and I think of change, how we must shed parts of ourselves to come out, stronger.

    I look at myself in the mirror, in the eyes, and I see the outline of my jaw brought forth by the setting sun, at the few pimples that line it, look at my nose, which is wide straight-on but pointed on the side, at the few blackheads that cave there, and I look at my eyes, at the skintags that home on my eyelids, and I look at my mouth, at the hair that grows above my upper lip, and I look at my face, at its roundness, and at my hair, at the oil that has already begun to form. And, taking this all in, as I am, I smile, and I lift a hand, press my palm to the glass, and I am beautiful. Exactly as I am, exactly as I come.

    This is what strength looks like.

Scars

I tell you I have scars, and yet you don't believe me. You shrug them off, and I don't blame you. Not really. My scars aren't as visible as most. In fact, they're not even visible from the surface, not one bit. They rest deep within me, carved into my heart, my lungs, my soul, and rarely do they shine through. They flicker among my eyes as I cast a look into the void of emotion and explain how exactly I got each scar. That's when people believe me, that's when people understand. But only for a brief glimpse of time before they forget, just like everyone else. I'm not sure why they forget, but I suppose it's because immediately after, my scars bury themselves back down and are replaced with a grin, a laugh. As though nothing happened, I carry on, and so do they, and my scars are never brought up again.

Unless, of course, they are forced to. You point a finger at me, tell me I'm wrong for having scars. Tell me I'm too happy to have scars. Too talented, too pretty. You tell me I am perfectly intact and have never felt pain. You call me nice. You call me sweet. And you laugh at me, and so do you, and so does everyone else, and you won't stop laughing, all of you. Eventually, the scars can't take any more threats to their existence and demand to be shown. They race up from down below, digging their claws into my throat and forcing themselves from my lips like flames, hot and in your face. They burn through my skin and bleed out lava, and you stare, and you watch, and you apologize. When you do, a smile twitches onto my face, and I laugh, and I forget, and so do you. And you invite everyone else to the party but me because I'm nice. Because I get quiet sometimes. I understand, I do.

The scars rest on my shoulders while I write, and only then do they feel most comfortable. When the sky is dark and the moon is shaded by the clouds and the right song drums in the background, they always come out to say hello, always kind, always supportive. They nuzzle against my neck and tell me what to write, teach me how to make my readers feel things in ways that I have. They're geniuses! They always know exactly what to do. Sometimes, they intertwine themselves within the words and take shelter among them, bleeding along the pages and bringing them to life.

If I could show my scars, I probably would, but they know their place, and so do I. They don't survive well in the daylight where others can see, so they take slumber during the day, and play with me only at night, while in slumber, or while I'm writing, or during the quiet moments in between the constant chaos. They protect me, they do. In fact, I enjoy having them around.

I just don't enjoy how I got them. I don't think anyone does.

Sometimes, you don't forget about my scars. Sometimes, you ask me how I'm doing, truly, and sometimes you care for me and sometimes, even, you love me. You see me for what I am, and you embrace me as I come. My scars, now comfortable, join us, propped up on my shoulder, one even sitting between us. I don't have to hide who I am, but the truth is, I never have. It is only my scars, protecting me, knowing their place. And me, smiling, understanding that my scars are difficult for others to carry, for others to see. My wall, it protects me from all of the things I fear. It'll come down eventually, don't worry. Just, not now.

I enjoy the moments when you remember my scars, acknowledge them. Realize that my smile, my laugh, isn't ingenious, but it's not who I am. No, not fully. When I get quiet, it's not because I don't like you, but because I have sunken, deep down, and I can't seem to get back up. No, not yet.

They're brief moments, when I am truly seen, but I enjoy them anyway.

Mending Her Own Tears

In a dark and gloomy woodland, Eden reflects on the past. Her back is leaned against a large oak tree and her wide eyes peer into the black fog, which blankets all she can see. She shivers against the night and watches as the full moon rolls into view above her head. It is much too late for someone like Eden to be in the woods, pondering, but in some odd way, she feels safest at night. No one can disturb her. No one can see her thoughts but herself.

Eden is thinking about Mathew again. Oh, how his face has never seemed to leave her mind, even an entire year later. She remembers the night as clear as ever, and she focuses on it with a wary heart and a trembling lip.

The kingdom threw their end-of-the-year ball, and as everyone expected, Mathew accompanied Eden. She linked her arm in his as they entered the castle, which had tall, eloquently painted ceilings and gold-plated walls with over-arching light fixtures bowing down to kiss the surrounding pillars. Eden clearly remembers the ballroom smelling like fresh lavender, warm cotton, and freshly baked cherry pies. As soon as they arrived, Mathew asked her to dance. How could she deny it? The night was marvelous, Eden in a white ball gown, her pointed ears decorated in her mother's finest jewels, and Mathew in a white tux to match Eden, his green skin less bright, more mature, as they say, beneath it. They danced for hours until it was time for dinner and drinks. They toasted with white wine and dined on roasted eel, simmered deer tongues, steamed vegetables from the kingdom's garden, fine, year-old cheeses made from the strongest bears the kingdom had, and newly plucked eyeballs from the neighboring goblins. For dessert, they ate cherry pie--she *knew* she smelled it-- with a side of buttered orc fingers. My, how delicious the meal was! The kingdom always prepared the finest meals.

When Mathew began talking to Lorelai, Eden's chest tightened. She knew they had a history, and although Mathew had never particularly mentioned her, Lorelai always seemed to sneer at Eden when they found themselves in the same place at the same time. Eden always had an off feeling about her, especially with her being near Matthew.

She trotted over and the two turned and welcomed Eden into their conversation. The weight hanging in Eden's chest lifted instantly, and together they laughed and sipped on their wine and eventually Mathew took Eden out to the dancefloor again.

Oh, how Mathew made her laugh. He was always there for her. Kind, gentle, affectionate. She was the only woman for him, he had told her, only a few months prior. He was to wed her, and they would live happily in a quiet cottage near a pond. They would be together, until the end.

Therefore, she didn't expect Mathew to run away with Lorelai at the end of the night.

When the ball had ended and waiters were clearing tables and sweeping the floor, Eden stood by herself in the corner, watching the happy couples and families depart and wondering where her date had gone. A friend explained in a sheepish tone that he had left early due to a stomachache, yet she couldn't help but notice Lorelai was absent as well. Having torn her dress on a chair while searching for Matthew, she excused herself to the restroom, only to not end up not fixing it at all, her trembling fingers unable to grasp at the needles she had brought in preparation, just in case. A knot swelled at her throat at the thought of Matthew gone, and possibly with Lorelai. She ended up lying there on the restroom floor, breathing deeply, pressing back the loud, angry thoughts. In the morning, her worst fear came alive when she went to visit Matthew with soup and juice for his stomach, only to find Lorelai scurrying out of his cottage.

Just two months later, Lorelai and Mathew married and soon after, had twin boys. Mathew didn't really give Eden an explanation. Not really. He simply told her he had fallen out of love with her--that Lorelai had something she didn't. He said it in the kindest way possible, but those words never do translate well.

Eden brings herself back to the dark forest around her and wipes her tears with a shaky hand. She knows she will heal. She knows she is still healing. At least, this is what everyone says.

She sits here now, her skin trembling against her bones, yet a strange warmth spreads about her. Somehow, beyond the emotions, she smiles to herself, because the more she stares out into the darkness, the more a figure begins to appear, and the more that figure begins to look like her, a few years from now, healthy and happy, full of life and no longer hurting. Eden reaches for that version of herself, sitting up a little straighter against the tree. Her future self leans down, embracing herself, grasping at her, tight, never letting go. At least, not fully. The image vanishes, but Eden can still feel herself holding on, tight.

Something in her heart, maybe her own voice, tells her to keep on moving. To let go and allow healing.

She *will* find someone new. The voice tells her so.

Sometimes people leave and start anew and while it pains, it is okay. All one can do from there is rise, move on, and embrace whatever comes next. An unusual happily ever after.

It is with this that her ragging thoughts dissipate, and she recognizes an urge to rest.
She obeys this inner command and stumbles back to her cozy cottage, her white nightgown taring on branches and bushes but otherwise staying intact, despite a few holes and rips.

Eden takes one last look at the bright moon, then heads inside and falls to sleep in her cot like a rock. It has been a long while since she's truly rested. Her aching memories are quiet at last.

In the morning, she sews her nightgown with calm, gentle hands.

I Know A Place

"I know a place," he told me. I didn't know him that well, had only met him a few moments before, but he seemed trustworthy for the most part. His face was kind, smooth, besides a streak of grime on his left cheek, his brown eyes brilliant with curiosity and thrill, something that was a rarity nowadays. He looked young, but not too young. He wore a black, tattered t-shirt and cargo pants that sat too large on his frame and I couldn't help but wonder if he had a family, or a mother to wipe up the grime. Of course, I didn't tell him he looked slightly ridiculous with a smudge on his cheek, but that was mostly because I couldn't. I felt sorry for him--I knew it was quite easy for a child to wind up lost in a world so ruined. He smiled widely at me and spun on his heels before slipping into the punctured air conditioning unit just to the right of him.

Practically rolling my eyes, but also deeply intrigued, I followed, sliding through the crack, sharp edges digging into my fur, my tail wisping behind me. He was waiting for me on the other side on all fours, and beamed at me when I appeared, as though he had a slight doubt that I wouldn't follow. As though he were used to others not following. "This way," he said, continuing forward into the tunnel, the dark encasing us. Luckily, I could see regardless, watching him crawl just a few spaces ahead of me. It smelled strongly of rust and chemicals.

Soon enough, we reached another door, and he kicked it down with his foot. Together, we slid out onto a ledge that barely fit him. In time, it would perhaps be too large, but at that moment it was fine and he walked along it with ease, with nearly perfect balance. Not as perfect as mine, though, but that's to be expected. My eyes peered over the edge to see the city lights below, descending down so far I could hardly see the end. The city itself lived indoors, in this vertical tunnel that extended deep into the ground, and had for quite some time, for as long as I had been alive. I had been informed that we are hiding from the beasts above, but I didn't know for sure. Above us, the illuminance radiated and casted a warm glow over all we could see. We were blanketed in the bright lights, which in a way were louder than the chattering of nearby people and the buzz of mechanics and tools every which way, using up all of our senses.

Eventually, we approached a pocket, which was shaded by the overhanging sidewalk above. We were practically invisible from everyone. I noticed a blanket dotted with tears and holes and a yellowed pillow that I presume once was white. He curled up against the blanket and tapped his hand against it, beckoning me to join him. I did, wrapping my tail around myself and nestling my side against his arm. He withdrew a new box of cigarettes from his pocket, most likely stolen, for cigarettes cost a fortune nowadays, as well as a lighter. He lit it easily, as though this was something he was familiar with and had done often. Inhaling deeply, he dropped the cigarette from his lips and exhaled white smoke into the air. He offered me some, and I neither accepted nor declined, for I couldn't really respond and he knew that.

"It's nice having some company for once," he said. "You know, even if you *are* just a cat." I blinked my eyes at him in agreement. For I, too, was a lone traveler in this desolate world. We sat up there for a long time, him and I. I came to enjoy him thoroughly at that moment. And I remained at his side for years to come, following him wherever he went. At that very moment, residing with him at that place for the first time, he became my friend.

I Will Remember You

In front of me stands a warrior from the kingdom of NightHill, his body completely covered with dented, yet otherwise in-tact black armor. His face is hidden behind a helmet so I cannot see whatever expression he may have. It's better this way. But even so, I assume his eyes weigh heavy on his face, imagine his lips dry and his teeth bared. He clutches his sword with a bandaged hand, his knuckles white as they wrap tighter around the handle. He trembles slightly from exhaustion, shudders against the cold, but otherwise stands tall and firm, one foot positioned before the other, his metal boots deep in the snow.

We are the last ones standing. Everyone else is either dead, sprawled out around us, or had fled long ago. We are in the white tundra, snow pouring down all around us, swept up by the wind and darting left and right, nearly knocking us off balance.

I face the soldier, holding my daggers with all the grip strength I have left. How long have we been fighting? Four hours? Maybe six? With the clouded, gray sky, hidden by the snowstorm, it's impossible to tell. My legs are weak and my calves burn with a fiery heat. My breathing has turned to sharp wheezes, my stomach completely empty and growling violently. My muscles twitch with hunger. But, I remain strong. As strong as I can be. And besides, he can't see the evident fatigue that crawls onto my face and settles there, not beneath the bright, red armor that covers me from head-to-toe. Nearly, at least; my armor is cracked on the right shoulder, revealing a deep wound from a sword that nearly chopped my arm clean off. The blood seeps out, collecting frost from the surrounding storm. Surprisingly, I hardly notice it.

If I kill him, StormValley takes over NightHill's kingdom. If he wins, NightHill takes over ours. Or is there even a winner at this point, with only two left? Would anyone even care, with the embarrassing number of soldiers who decided to run away for shelter?

Nonetheless, I made a vow to my kingdom the day I became a soldier: I would continue to fight as though my life depended on it. And in this moment, it does.

He takes a step toward me, and I clutch my daggers tighter. He lifts his sword, panting heavily. I see his shoulders quake against the movement, and then he swings at me. Fast. Hard. I leap out of the way and aim my dagger at his side. He dodges, swings again. And I roll away from him, aiming for his throat. He pounces away from me. And again, he swings, and I aim, and we're rotating around each other, our panting loud and our movements pathetically slow. The wind is harsh around us, pulling us closer to one another. The entire world is a blur, as though it is only us that exist. Both fighting for our kingdoms. Fighting for our lives.

He takes another step toward me, and the earth cracks beneath him. Frantically, he retreats, but this only causes the earth to tremble then reveal an opening. The snow and ice open beneath his feet and he falls deep into the darkness. I hear him *smack* against the rock, and then I hear nothing.

I don't know what to do. He's probably dead. And to my astonishment, I don't feel happy about it. Instead, I feel a deep pit flourish in my stomach. *Do I... feel for him? Feel for this warrior who just tried to kill me, most likely killed many of my friends during battle? He didn't even have a real chance at fighting me.*

Before I can truly process what I'm feeling, the earth roars, then shatters beneath me and I fall after him, slamming against the hard, cavern floor. I smash my hip into a rock, and hot pain shoots up my side. My wrist, too, which was used to stupidly stop my fall, bends backward and *snaps*, causing my arm to stiffen and flood with an agonizing sting. After a brief moment of shock, a scream rises from my chest and echoes about the cave. I roll onto my back and rip off my helmet, thick tears seeping out from my eyes. I clutch my broken wrist with my good hand, feeling the intense throb of my left hip caress my entire body with sharp throbs.

"Sucks, didn't it?" rasps the NightHill warrior from behind me. His voice is deep, but I can tell that he is young. My eyes dart to meet his, and just as they do, he takes off his helmet. His dark eyes harden and his teeth grit, masking the pain. He forces the corners of his mouth up into a grin, perhaps trying to add humor to this dreadful situation. My eyes then dip down to see his leg, which bends the opposite way in front of him. Feeling queasy at the sight, I lift my eyes to meet his face again.

"Y-yeah," I say. I roll my head back to lie flatly on the ice, looking up at the gray sky which peaks out from the hole we formed in the earth. A moan forces itself from my lips as I tremble against the pain, the expanding weakness. I notice that my vision begins to blur, the air harder to breathe in.

"My name is Cade," he says. He stirs and groans softly as he does.

"We are still enemies," I spat.

"C-certainly," he says. "Wha-what is your name?" It is silent for a moment before he stirs again then gasps. "Oh, *god*, holy... *Goddamn*! This... *sucks*!" he cries. However, oddly enough, I can sense a pang of humor in his voice. For some reason, this makes me chuckle. Just a bit. *So, he's funny*, I think.

"If I told you my name," I wheeze, containing myself, "I don't know if I could kill you anymore. I'd make things more personal than they have become."

"No need to worry about that," he tells me. "We'll die naturally soon enough. I doubt anyone will come for us."

I sigh heavily, my entire body now pulsating with a heated ache. "Fine. M-My name is... Myla." Words become harder to say, turning to mush in my mouth.

"It... it's nice to meet you... Myla."

I smile slightly to myself, despite the pounding heartbeat that settles beneath my skin all over. "You... too, Cade."

We lie there in silence, each of us groaning separately, our voices being carried off into the depth of the cavern. The winds howl above us, creating a somewhat peaceful sound now that we're beneath the storm. My eyes watch the flakes of snow wisp past and occasionally sprinkle down into the cave and onto my armor. Then suddenly, an intense wave of panic overcomes me as I think, *Am I going to die here? Is this truly the end?* Yet the thought, even the feeling, is fleeting. Over the years, I've learned how to overcome any fear or worry regarding death. I have to be brave against it as a warrior. In fact, I've prepared for this moment my entire life. Well, not *this* moment, and in this exact way, but rather acceptance. When we vow to be a soldier, we vow to die in battle.

Although, now that it's come, I can't help but wonder why. Why I spent all these years fighting for my kingdom, why I devoted my life to a man who spends the entirety of his day on a throne, safe. Why didn't I instead… *live*? Surely, there has to be more to life than war.

My eyes flicker back to Cade. He's already staring at me, a gentle smirk on his lips and sweat beading on his forehead despite the chill around us. A puddle of blood forms around his leg, seeping out from beneath him, but I try not to look and instead focus on his eyes. His eyes are kind, shielding the intense agony within. When I see his face, think of his name, I can't imagine him as an enemy anymore. I can't imagine him as the warrior who moments before was trying to kill me. I only see him as a person simply fighting for a kingdom he trusts. Like me. And he's young. So young. No older than twenty-one. But who am I to call someone young? I'm nineteen.

"Are you... afraid to...to die?" I croak. I'm surprised at myself for asking him this. But then again, I'm not.

His face sinks in, just a bit, but then he smiles. Laughs, even. "No," he says without hesitation. "But... but you know what I... am afraid of? My kingdom... failing...be-because of me." His eyes flicker away, his smile swept off his face and now replaced with gritted teeth. "But... do you know... what's funny about... that? I... doubt... anyone from my kingdom... will even remember... my name."

"I'll... remember... your name, Cade," I say.

His eyes float to mine and linger there, and he smiles. "And I'll... remember... yours, Myla."

Mother and I

My paws sink into the snow as I tread behind Mother. White flakes rush down from the fogged sky, clouding our vision, but we progress regardless. We're hungry. Starved, more like it. Our bodies rattle against the cold, despite the thickness and natural warmth of our fur, as we search for any possible prey. Well, as Mother searches for any possible prey. I stay behind, old enough to make a kill but still dependent on Mother's sharp reflexes. I keep my eyes low, searching the snow and bare spaces of dirt for any sign of life, but this desolate world is silent, besides the roar of the wind and Mother and I's pants and occasional groans against the bitter chill of the air. We're used to this though--we have to be.

Suddenly, Mother stops, almost frozen, and twitches her gaze to a nearby tree, barren and caked with snow. Moments after, I hear it too--a faint, small, and barely audible footstep, just one. It knows we are near, so we must be careful, and patient. Mother dips her head to the earth, so quiet my pants remain louder than her movements. She lifts a paw, barely setting it down in front of her, not making a single sound. She continues to prowl onward, toward the sound, and I follow after her, moving slightly to the left to limit the prey's ability to escape. We move slowly, yet silent, our coats damped with snow, which has turned our black-spotted coat into a perfectly white camouflage. My yellow eyes narrow in at the base of the tree, my face tight and my mouth moistening as the smell of hare becomes more prominent. My stomach trembles with hunger as we near, closer.

The hare leaps from the snow and races into the white horizon. Mother and I pounce after it, running at full speed into the snowstorm. The hare blends in well into its surroundings, but we can still hear it, we can still smell it, and so we follow its tail without much difficulty. Our pants are loud against the wind, but we don't need to worry about staying silent anymore. I near the hare, but allow Mother to catch it, as she catches far more than I. She gains up on it, snatches it with her teeth in one attempt, and then it is ours.

Mother carries the hare as we journey back to our cave, and it is the most challenging walk for both of us, as the scent of fresh hare overwhelms our senses. If we could, we would eat it there, but we must hide it, for others may come and take it in this forsaken world, where prey is terribly scarce. I watch the lifeless hare dangle from Mother's jaw, marveling at the idea that this animal was once alive, and now it is our dinner. In some strange way, I feel sad for it.

When we arrive at the cave, we settle onto the cold earth, our tails wrapping tightly around ourselves, enveloping us in its warmth, and we tear into our dinner. It's not much, but it's enough, for now. Soon, after just mere moments, the meat is gone, and Mother and I gnaw on the bones. Together, we watch the snow continue to fall, creating large piles outside the cave opening and settling into the crevices between the rock. I think about other animals living among this harsh world, and wonder how they are doing, if they've survived this year's harsh winter so far. I think about my brother, who was left behind on a hunt months ago, and I wonder if he has survived, if he has started a family of his own. In time, I will have to leave Mother, and the thought frightens me terribly. My mind cannot stop racing and then I think about the hares and wonder if they miss the one we just killed. I wonder if he had a name. A family. I thank the hare and its family in my mind, accepting that it has already been done. You must be okay with death in this world. Death creates the cycle.

      Mother leans in toward me, rests her head on mine, and heaves out a hefty sigh of relief, and my thoughts melt into a warming relief. All I truly know is that right now, Mother and I are safe, and full.

Going on A Walk

I step out of my house at 6:33 a.m. exactly. Twenty-seven minutes early. Not bad.

The office complex where I work is only a mile or so away. I like to walk there; it's always my favorite part of the day. I've always liked walks, and it's hard to explain why, so I won't go into too much detail, because my intention is not to bore you. Not at all.

The air outside is dewy, but it's clean and crisp, too; I breathe it in and feel refreshed. It's a bit cloudy and the sun, which is still easing up from beyond the horizon, is mostly hidden. A few sun rays leak out anyways and coat random things like every other tree or small patches along the sidewalk.

I situate my coat and stuff one hand in my pocket, the other clutching my briefcase, and I start my usual, everyday stroll. Did I mention that it's quite chilly? It's November, and the leaves have mostly fallen to the earth, and the air is not cold enough to be considered cold, although it's not warm enough to where it'd be comfortable without a jacket, at least. Ideal weather in my opinion--I can breathe it in without my lungs freezing, but I still have to wear a coat because when it grazes my bare skin, I shiver. I prefer cloudy days over sunny days, too, and I don't know why because I'm not one to enjoy melancholy things or darkness, yet I feel more productive on days when the sun isn't blazing into my eyes, on days when I'm not vulnerable to everyone else. I hate feeling vulnerable. I hate it. I'd prefer to keep my head low with my body mostly covered and that's all, really.

My shoes are loud against the pavement, and besides the occasional bird chirps, the sound of footsteps is all I can hear. No one is really awake yet. Or, at least, no one is walking outside. People are piling into cars, still half asleep with heavy bags beneath their eyes, their hair still wet from their quick showers. They look at me walking and kind of frown because I'm walking and they're driving and they envy me, yet at the same time, they don't; they feel somewhat superior. Everyone is always driving and thinking that driving is cooler and I'm not sure why they do that. I'm not sure why people are the way that they are. I just ignore them or watch from afar.

It's not that I'm antisocial or hate people because I like people very much. They're so fascinating, really. They really are. I see a person now. He is standing outside of his apartment on his balcony, leaning against the side of the building with a cup of coffee in one hand and nothing in the other. His other hand is just hanging there awkwardly like it doesn't really know what to do. *He* doesn't really know what to do. His hair is a mess and his eyes are staring off to somewhere else, somewhere far from here. He's wearing pajama pants and a light t-shirt and his feet are bare and I wonder whether or not he's cold. It looks like he's avoiding the inside of his house, avoiding something that's going on within. *There's no escape*, he says to himself. *This is it.*

He glances at me and sees me staring, then turns to go back inside.

I am nearing the shops and I know this because I can hear the people that stumble between them. They're all wearing suits like me and the majority are carrying briefcases. There is a woman running, too, and another woman is pushing a small child in a stroller, but usually, people do not wake up this early to do anything but get to work.

There are scattered puddles in the road. Cars drive past and graze them with their wheels, and water is splashed up onto the sidewalks and occasionally the water will get on my pants, but I don't mind it.

I stop near one of the puddles and look down into it and stare at myself. I look at my face and wonder why it looks the way it does, why it must be so strangely squared and pale. Why are my eyes brown and dark and why can't they be green or blue or anything a tad more colorful? Why must my lips be so small?

I think like this sometimes without meaning to and it's really bad that I do. And I mean *really* bad. Thoughts like this do me no good, especially early in the morning when my mind is still fuzzy and the day is still young, because during this time the seeds planted have a greater chance of flourishing, since the soil is so soft. It doesn't matter which seeds are planted, either. You could grow roses or venus flytraps, it's really up to you.

Why people talk bad to themselves, I seriously don't know, because the body is so delicate and it could shatter at the slightest of touches. Think about it: People fall by the simplest things, and they fall all the time. A few negative words spoken by someone close can make any receiver feel as though they are living in a rotting casket for weeks or even months. If we are angry at others for being rude to us, why aren't we angry at *ourselves* for being rude to us? It doesn't make sense, not in the slightest. But then again, nothing does. No matter how many times someone explains to me why the sky is blue or why the word love can be used too much or why good foods are always the worst for you or why we are on a floating ball in space, it'll never make sense. Not really.

I lift my head and continue walking.

The town is lovely, and that's why I moved here. Not necessarily for the job, but for the scenery. The trees are tall and luscious, even in the fall; their leaves are large and carry all sorts of magnificent colors, like orange and yellow and red and all of the colors you'd expect to see, and the leaves are always speckled with fresh dew and bursting with liveliness. At least, this is true for the few that remain on the branches, for most have fallen already.

The buildings are made from gray stone, and the sidewalks are paved with the same gray stone, and the entire town seems to be a perfect place for any aspiring author to just move to and stay for a while. The streets are lined with coffee shops and bookstores and boutiques and florists and small-town markets. Not many families live here, but there's always women with strollers and small children anyways.

I pause by my favorite coffee shop and step inside. It's partially crowded like it always is, an average-sized line forming by the counter. I add myself to the line, and while waiting to order, I find myself watching the baristas behind the counter. One is brewing coffee, one is making drinks, and one is working the cashier. All three of them look tired, but they're nice anyway, and they smile at people when making accidental eye-contact. They're not genuinely happy, however, like they portray themselves to be. All three of them stayed up late the night before, probably worrying over relationships or school or something that probably won't matter a year from now, but they don't know that yet because they haven't experienced enough to truly believe it. I want to reach out to them and assure them that it's alright and that they don't need to worry anymore, and that they should never worry again because life is too short for that. Although, if I *did* decide to reach out, they'd think I'm strange or crazy and they wouldn't really do anything except smile and hand over my coffee.

    I order a plain, black coffee with just a little room for cream, and when I pour in my cream I watch it explore the darkness like a curious child dancing among the unknown. The cream twirls about the coffee, extending into the black. Over time, the coffee turns to a deep tan, and the cream itself disappears completely because it is now a part of the coffee. I forget that the cream is even there, and I feel sorry for the cream because it was curious and that's all--it didn't mean to lose itself along the way. It never does.

    I leave the coffee shop and continue toward my work.

    Next door to the coffee shop is a bookstore, and outside of the bookstore sits a bed of flowers. The flowers are yellow and pink and they're dying, their spines twisting and curling and their heads arching over and facing down toward the soil. At this moment, I wonder why the most beautiful things in life, like flowers, must be some of the first to die. Why they're plucked from the earth and laid out to wither away. Why the cold air grips their necks so firmly and doesn't really touch anything else. It's not fair, really, that the natural beauties of life must be so fragile. This is it; this is their life--to be beautiful, an eye-catcher, and that is all. Of course, they contribute many other things, but those things are often overlooked because people only really look at outside beauty.

    I stare at the flowers a little longer and I wonder why life is the way it is. Why do plants grow, and why do they just sit still and watch us? Do they enjoy their lives as we do? And, where do they come from? Or, at least, why from the dirt? Why from the ground, and why not from the sky? Who decided such things? Who was given the permission to plan out the way the world was supposed to work?

    Life is such an odd thing. It really is. And who decided to name it "Life", anyway? Who created the English language, and how?

    I lift my head and blink my eyes a few times and for a moment, everything around me is blurry, and then it isn't. I continue on my way through the streets and wonder why I always think of such peculiar things, and I also wonder why I'm always wondering, anyway, because too much wondering doesn't do anyone any good. But, at

195

the same time, too little wondering leads for such a boring life.

I glance at an older woman's face and I try to figure out whether or not she wonders too little, too much, or just enough? However, what, in this case, would be the correct amount of wondering? Maybe, perhaps, I'm the only one who wonders.

I sip on my coffee delicately because it has finally become comfortably warm against my palm. I taste the creamy, flavor and let it fester on my tongue before entirely swallowing it down.

There are so many sensations, all of the time, and it's a shame that some people cannot see that. In the end, life is not about what is to come in the future, and what has occurred in the past, but it is about what is dwelling in this current moment, and what is drawing the most attention. The people or the buildings or the flowers or the coffee or even *you*; it could be anything. Life is about understanding what is most important to oneself in the current moment, and while it's challenging sometimes, controlling these thoughts in this manner is the only true way one could comfortably get by.

God, I can ramble. But, it's true anyhow. It's all so true that it hurts, like a hard slap to the face. Life is this extending vortex, filled with thoughts and perceptions of time and emotions that aren't really there but are actually allusions and every little problem we've ever faced has never really occurred because we aren't truly here, we are somewhere else. The vortex gets brighter and deeper as you fall forevermore into the depths of your mind, and only once you allow your thoughts to leak in through the cracks, will you be able to settle.

I am finished with my coffee, and this is funny because I don't remember drinking all of it so quickly. The taste barely remains on my tongue, almost as if the coffee was never there at all. The people around me return to their normal paces and their faces become normal and everything goes normal again and stays that way.

A sudden urge tells me to stop walking, and I glance up to see my office complex. I toss away the empty coffee cup and walk through the glass doors at 6:54 a.m., somewhat exhausted, but somewhat ready. And I realize, as I walk through these doors, that it is only during times like this, in the early hours of the day and amidst the morning air, when my mind wanders so far and wide, and perhaps this is why I enjoy walking to work.

The Night I Saw Him One Last Time

I am old now. So, why I was called to the carnival where the children played, where my family and I once had gone quite frequently but not for years, not since the happening, I had no idea. But, my gut, the voices, or some unknown force pulled me, urging me to go, and since I had nothing planned that evening, I followed it.

Beneath the vibrant, fluttering illuminance, I saw him. He was standing directly across from me, beside the Ferris wheel, arms limp at his sides, dark eyes boring into mine. Besides this, he looked normal, as though it was just yesterday when it happened, his white blonde hair a curly, unkempt mess atop his head, a faded black t-shirt too loose on his lanky frame, his jeans a bit too long and frayed at the ends where they met the wet concrete beneath him, his white sneakers muddied. He never truly cared how people saw him, or if he looked presentable, and yet he remained handsome, and people were constantly drawn to him. Everyone loved him. And I envied him for it. More so, I hated it. In fact, I hated *him*, with everything I had, the sight of him always creating a ball of fiery heat in my chest when I was younger, my palms clammy, my mouth dry. I could never live up to him, even after everything I had done in my life.

But in that moment, at the carnival, the sight of him froze me in time, the people and the lights and the carnival music all but blurs to my ears. Everything, even my heart, stopped, as I stared straight into his eyes, and I saw the corners of his lips curl, quite unnaturally, into a grin. Friendly, inviting. Then, he stepped toward me through the crowds, his eyes never leaving me. And, soon enough, he was there, gazing down at me. His skin looked worn, and he had new wrinkles which had blossomed around the corners of his lips. His hand stretched out toward me, chapped along the knuckles, and although I hesitated briefly, as it had been so long since I last saw him, I grabbed it, shocked that he was there, that I could feel him, that he was real, and I vanished alongside him into the crowd.

    First, as we had always done before, he and I visited the cotton candy vendor, his favorite. He watched as I bit into the sugary, pink fluff, laughing at me when I got bits of it stuck on my chin, leaving a sticky residue. I paused, glanced up at him, and I asked him how he found me, and he grinned and said, You weren't too difficult to find. And so, I asked why he waited so long, then, because we are both so grown up now, and he said, I had to wait for the right time, when we were ready. Besides this, we didn't talk much. He told me he already knew everything about me, as he had been a silent observer, apparently watching my life pass from the shadows, and yet, I had never noticed his presence until now. When I asked him how he had been, where he had gone, what he saw there, he told me, You have to wait to see for yourself. But I can assure you, you'll quite like it.

We left the cotton candy vendor and sauntered throughout the fair, watching little children giggle wildly as they raced past us and remembering when we were once that small, that innocent. We approached a ring toss carnival game, and I won myself a little, pink teddy bear. After this, he urged us to visit the haunted house, something we were never allowed to do previously. It was quite a small, unassuming building made of mirrored rooms and clowns, now chipping away, painted on the exterior, but it was fun anyway. Surprisingly, I found that he was more afraid than I, as we traversed through.

Lastly, for old time's sake, we rode the Ferris wheel, snuggled up side-by-side, and I laid my head on his shoulder as we propelled upward into the sky. I felt the air on my cheeks and asked if he could and he said, No, but I can feel you. And I said, I can feel you, too. When we got to the top, we gazed down at the town, brought forth by the few warm lights dotted along the valleys. The summer air felt humid and clung to me but since it was night, it was refreshingly cool, especially when the breezes wisped through my hair. I asked him when I'd see him again and he said, Who's to say? And I said, I hate that you're so vague, and he laughed, and then I asked him, Why me? And he turned to me, perplexed, one eyebrow lifted. And so, I went on to say, You hated me, didn't you? And I hated you, too. We… were terrible to each other. And he laughed, and his laugh was silent, just like him. He told me, calmly, That's precisely why it's you. You were the only one who saw me through my bullshit. Who saw me as I was. But I was mean to you, I said. That's what siblings do, he told me. Then, he continued, I'm sorry I wasn't a better older brother. I'm sorry I was never there. And I said, You're here now. He leaned over and held me, and I held back, hard, my fingers curling into his stiff shirt, breathing in his always-too-strong-cologne, and I pressed into him, closer, never wanting to let go, wanting to hold onto this moment forever, until he vanished beneath my grip.

When the Ferris wheel descended, I got off alone. But this wasn't shocking to anyone, I'm sure. And then, I walked home, with a smile on my face and the teddy bear in my grasp.

The Girl with The Book

When she walks in, she immediately catches my eye. She's not someone you'd think that would catch my eye, but she does. Her eyes are wide and a deep, warm brown, her brown hair wavy around her face, falling down her back like water. Her features are sharp, but unique. She wears neutral clothes that sit loosely around her frame and she clutches onto her purse with both hands, presumably unsure of what to do with either of them. She bites her lip, scans the room, then continues toward the counter to order. A bright smile slides onto her face with ease as she greets the cashier, which in turn encourages the cashier to politely smile back. They laugh at something, and her giggle slices through the quiet air and settles there. It isn't annoying like most people's laughs are. It welcomes an openness to the air, a friendless that finds comfort in the corners of the room. She orders something, pays, and as she does, drops her credit card and somehow kicks the counter with her boot. Sheepishly, she apologies, bending down to pick up her card and for a brief moment, unsure where the card is even supposed to go. She has to ask but asks with a chuckle as though it's funny. She's clumsy and doesn't try to hide it. When she's done paying, she walks over to the other side of the counter with her arms crossed, pressing her lips together. She finds a corner and settles into it, patiently waits for her coffee. Her eyes search the sea of faces in the cafe, observing, thinking. Her friendly expression has been swept off her face and has been replaced with an expression of wonder and curiosity, one that I have only seen on a child's. *What could she be thinking about?* I wonder.

I realize I've been staring too long and glance back to my book. She wouldn't notice me if I continued looking, as she is evidently oblivious to most surroundings, more concerned with what's in her head, but *still*. I pick up where I left off, lifting my mug of green tea to my lips, taking a sip of the lukewarm, bitter liquid. A warmth spreads throughout me, exactly what I needed on such a cold, snowy day.

"A latte for Brittney!?" the barista shouts. My eyes dart up to see her press a strand of hair behind her ear, smile softly, and take the coffee. She spins on her heels and searches for an available seat. Although there are several, she takes an awfully long time to decide. Her fingers lift to her mouth and she gnaws on her thumb nervously. Eventually, she walks over to a high-top table by the window and slides in, draping her purse over the chair and pulling out a book. I almost can't believe that she fit an entire book into that small purse. I notice that the pages are bent and scrunched, part of the cover folded over. She doesn't seem to care about this, gently smoothing back the cover and the pages, prying open the book, and stuffing her nose deep into the pages. One hand hovers over her mouth as she chews on her nails, one by one. I wonder if she knows that she should stop biting her nails. She probably does. Maybe she doesn't mind it.

Part of me considers walking over to say hello. She seems about my age and is the only person at the cafe not scrolling on their phone and instead, immersed in a story. It's refreshing to see someone so intrigued in a story. We're a lot alike-I can already tell, just by watching her. She doesn't think that anyone else notices her, but they do. I do. I sip my tea, which now is room temperature, nearly too cool to enjoy anymore. I sigh, returning to my book and deciding against saying anything. She wouldn't be interested in a guy like me, anyway. I can already tell. She's independent, doesn't care what others think of her, doesn't care about the latest trends or styles. She just… is. Spending her Saturday afternoon alone in a coffee shop, reading a book.

    After about an hour, she stands up from the chair and collects her things, sliding the book back into her purse and finishing up her latte. She places the empty mug in the bin near the door, then without even glancing back, leaves the cafe. I watch the girl with the book walk away, clutching her purse with both hands, until she vanishes into the city crowd, becoming just another face beneath the fall of the snow.

The Most Interesting Man I've Ever Met

I've only ever met one man I'd truly call interesting. He lived directly above my apartment and his name was Jimbo-Jee Patterson. He told people to call him Pat, but as his downstairs neighbor, I could call him Jimbo. When I first saw him, he was moving in. None of his clothes matched and were all a little too tight. He had a small, hot pink, rolling suitcase, and a backpack, as though he were leaving to board a flight and was planning to only stay a single night. He was older than most people living in the complex, as it was located downtown and near the popular bars. White hairs poked out from his baseball cap and skin sagged around his eyes. Standing in my doorway, watching him climb the stairs, I asked if he wanted help, and he politely declined.

"This is all I have, but thank you, Son."

I couldn't believe that was *all* he had, but I restricted myself from questioning him. I nodded once, then returned to my small, studio apartment. It wasn't much, just a few movie posters on the walls and a futon, which doubled as a bed, positioned next to the refrigerator--its hum, I discovered, relaxed me and helped me fall asleep—and a pile of disparaged comics and books.

The balcony is what won me over. It overlooked the entire city and was large enough for a small table and two chairs. I spent my life out on that balcony. It was my escape from everything, especially at night when the city lights beamed and danced wildly in the distance. I was only three stories up, but from where I stood on the balcony, I felt as though the entire world was at my fingertips.

When Jimbo moved in above me, my little paradise became much less quiet. He was noisy and always had people over, all day and all night. And at around two in the morning, everyone left except a girl, maybe two, and I wouldn't be able to sleep. Even the refrigerator hum couldn't overpower the rowdy insanity of Jimbo.

It took me two weeks to build up the courage and tell him to quiet down. I knocked on his door and within a few seconds, he burst it open, a wild smile on his face. To my surprise, no one was home, but then again it was eight in the morning.

"Coffee?" he asked before I could even speak, my fist still mid air from knocking. I glanced Jimbo up and down and saw that he was wearing nothing but a red and black, plaid robe and fuzzy, wool socks. His white chest hair stuck out all over and although I felt uncomfortable entering his apartment, I nodded.

His place was identical to mine, except everything was bright and mix-matched and honestly, his decorating skills looked like hell. But I could tell by a simple sweep of my eyes that this place was his. It was him in an apartment. String lights hung from all over and he didn't have a table, just a bunch of bean-bags and I found myself wondering, *when did he bring up the rest of his stuff?*

He poured the darkened coffee into a yellow coffee cup and when he asked if I wanted cream or sugar, I told him I liked it black. I took a singular sip and still remember the smoky bitterness that overwhelmed my senses. It was most certainly the best cup of coffee I've ever had in my life.

While I gulped down the roasted goodness, settled in a purple bean-bag chair, Jimbo proceeded to tell me his life story. He grew up in a small town in India and traveled the entire world before he turned five. "I wish I could remember any of it," he told me, laughing. He and his family then moved to America. Ohio of all places. He grew up as a normal child, attending grade school, playing soccer outside with his neighbors. That is, until his parents got divorced because his dad had been cheating heavily, and so his mom moved him to San Francisco at the age of fifteen. He had no friends and was badly bullied and spent his free time alone. His mother began dating bad guys and those bad guys were mean to Jimbo and eventually, after two years in San Francisco, he gathered enough from money mowing lawns and ran away and flew to his old house in Ohio where he thought his dad still resided. But the house was gone. Within the past year, the entire neighborhood had been knocked down and replaced with a strip-mall in-progress. He didn't have his dad's number-- his mom never gave it to him. So, from there, Jimbo moved to Cleveland and lived on the streets. His mother never called, and the police never came looking, so he was on his own for quite some time. He met a homeless man named Rob who slept on the same street Jimbo did. Rob became his new father figure and is the only reason Jimbo is alive today. When Rob died, Jimbo was eighteen and joined a bad crowd because he had nowhere else to go. About a year into drug dealing, he was caught and thrown in jail and was there for seven years. He got out at twenty-six and decided to change his life. He worked his way from a McDonald's dishwasher to a photographer and then a videographer and five years later he became one of the world's best directors of all time. He made lots of money and met lots of famous people and was married twice, both of which ended rather nicely. "They were both sweet, pretty girls. Our spark just faded, I suppose," he had said with a faraway look in his eyes. He vows to never cheat on a woman, like his dad did. And now, he's here, a sixty-year-old videographer hippie, no longer a director, who never settles in the same place for more than a month. He told me that he'd been planning to move to San Francisco in just a week in hopes of finding his mom, whom he has yet to speak to since running away.

"So, neighbor, what'd you come here for?" he asked me directly after finishing his life story.

My jaw unhinged, I stared at him blankly, my coffee cup empty and lying awkwardly in my lap. "Oh, well… I'm so sorry, but what was your name?"

"Jimbo-Jee Patterson," he said proudly. "My friends call me Pat, but as my upstairs neighbor, you can call me Jimbo."

Of course, his name is Jimbo, I thought.

"Do you… well, *Jimbo*… do you mind keeping it down at night? You're a bit loud, all the time…."

He laughed so hard he slipped out of his bing-bag. This surprised me greatly and on instinct I frantically reached out toward him, but he swatted me away, half-lying on the floor, his privates nearly exposed. "Why, of course!" Then, he paused, stared at me deeply. "Why don't you come to my party tonight?"

And so, without much hesitation, since I didn't have many friends of my own, I agreed. I had secretly been yearning to attend a party. And I went to the next one, and the next one, and every other party Jimbo threw before leaving for San Francisco. Every night there were different people, different girls, and I had no earthly clue where anyone came from or how they knew or were related to Jimbo. Everyone seemed normal, plain, boring, including myself--*especially* myself-- but all together in Jimbo's place, we came alive.

I still miss Jimbo. It's been a couple months since he's moved, and I haven't heard anything from him--he doesn't and won't ever own a phone or social media. He said this to me as we said goodbye but promised that he would write, when he felt like it, and in one quick spin-around, he trotted away with his hot-pink suitcase and backpack.

My new upstairs neighbor is quiet and to himself, so my balcony has gone back to the simple little paradise I've always loved. The parties were nice, but I had certainly craved my moments of solitude.

Even so, I hope Jimbo has reunited with his mom, and I do hope he writes to me soon. I doubt I'll ever meet anyone quite like him again.

Too Good for Me

I have a boyfriend who is much too good for me. I'm crying because I ate too many brownies and his arms wrap around my shoulders and pull me closer into him like it's the most normal thing in the world to cry about overeating. I'm stressed because my writing is crap and I drop my head in my hands and he walks over and lifts my chin and looks me in the eyes and tells me that my writing is the best crap he's ever read. I'm overwhelmed by forty-eight things and he scoops up all forty-eight things like they're really nothing, and they *are* but they matter to me and he knows that and so he sits with me and together, we sort them out, every single nothing, one at a time. I'm panicking because I don't want to be touched there and he retreats immediately and he listens and he kisses my cheek, my earlobe, and tells me that I'm okay, that I'm *safe*.

I had a boyfriend who shared my sense of humor and made me laugh until my stomach ached and joyful tears swelled in my eyes. He danced with me, one hand settled on my waist and one cupping the back of my neck and he looked down at me and told me I was the most beautiful girl he had ever seen in his entire life. He held my hand at the mall and never let it go and I felt proud, as though I was honored to be next to him and not the other way around. One time, he kissed me in the hallways at school and everyone saw me with him and everything was perfect but *oh*, how I thought he was too good for me, at that time.

I had a boyfriend who I thought was too good for me until I met my current boyfriend. I cried because I ate too many brownies and he told me I was being annoying. I was stressed because my writing was crap and he shrugged and told me he had to return to his video game and he never once read anything I wrote. I was overwhelmed by forty-eight things and so he gave me space. I panicked because I didn't want to be touched there and he touched me anyway and said "this is ridiculous" when I told him "no" a second time.

I have a boyfriend who is much too good for me but reminds me that I'm much too good for him and therefore, in our opinion, it cancels out. We make each other laugh until our stomachs ache and joyful tears swell our eyes. We dance together in the comforting darkness of my bedroom and we look at each other and admire one another and not *just* because of our looks but because of who we are. We hold hands and not because we're each other's prize but because we like feeling each other's clammy skin against our own, feeling connected to one another, feeling synchronized. And sometimes we kiss in public but not for everyone to see, but for us, a silent message of love that only we can hear.

Loose Threads

I.

For the longest time, I had been holding onto you with nothing but a loose thread, that loose thread being "best friend". You were my best friend. Right? Yes, *right*. I could feel you slipping, and so my grasp tightened because you were my best friend. I would text you and later that evening I'd get a short reply and an apology for the late response and I'd say that's ok, because you're my best friend and I'm your best friend and I know you care for me. You'd tell me you were busy that week and had no time to hang out and then I'd hear your laugh echo and I'd see that you weren't, in fact, busy, but participating in other activities, with other people, but I'd ignore it and my grasp would tighten, and tighten, and my fingers would blister and my skin would burn and then *you* ended up letting go, and I watched the thread fall to the floor, my hands bloodied and bruised and empty for the first time in a long time.

What now?

II.

I've always wanted a best friend. Not just a boyfriend, perhaps because in the past, boyfriends were unreliable and I haven't quite healed from that. But, who knows for sure. I've always chased it, this idea of a forever friend. And I don't just mean someone to have sleepovers with, someone to gossip with, someone to paint my nails and take me shopping and vice versa. I've always craved closeness, *intense* closeness, where we tell each other anything and everything, even our darkest secrets, even our worst fears, and we guide each other through life, through relationships and heartbreak, friends until the grave. We cry together and cling tightly and *love* each other through thick and thin, through anything. I want someone to see me to my fullest, to see my flaws and my mistakes and my intensity and accept it, all of it. I want to make sure I'm not alone, and I want to be someone's soulmate, their other half. I want to be thought of, wanted, needed.

And this entire time, while I've been chasing this want, hoping and praying for the perfect person to show up in my life and ease my swelling loneliness, I've been standing right there, staring at my reflection but looking slightly past my own eyes. I've sat alone in my bedroom at night and wished for the comfort of a person, forgetting that I have hands, a voice, a smile, a mind of my own.

I already am my own best friend.

And yet, I want more. I cannot be enough for myself.

III.

Why did you leave me? Did I say the wrong thing? Do I smile too much? Do I come across as fake, or mean, or annoying, or stupid, or full of myself, or too nice, or too loud, or too quiet? Am I too honest? Do I talk too much? Did I bother you? Tell me, please, and I'll fit into your mold. I'll shrink down into your perfect friend, and I'll say what you want me to say, and I'll support you in any way that I can, and I'll reach out first, and I'll buy you gifts, and I'll care for you so much. I've done it before and I can do it again.

It still won't be enough. You'll still leave.

Even if I do everything right, they always leave.

Why did you leave? Why did you leave? Why did you leave? Why did you leave? Why did you leave? Why did you leave? Why did you leave? Why did you leave? Why does everyone keep leaving me? Why did you leave? Why did you leave? Why did you leave? Why did you leave? Why did you leave? Why did you leave? Why did you leave? Why did you leave? Why did you leave? Why did you leave? Why did you leave? Why does everyone keep leaving me? Why did you leave? Why did you leave? Why did you leave? Why did you leave? Why did you leave? Why did you leave? Why did you leave? Why did you leave? Why did you leave? Why did you leave? Why does everyone keep leaving me? Why did you leave? Why did you leave? Why did you leave? Why did you leave? Why did you leave? Why did you leave? Why did you leave? Why did you leave? Why did you leave? Why did you leave? Why does everyone keep leaving me? Why did you leave? Why did you leave? Why did you leave? Why did you leave? Why did you leave? Why did you leave? Why did you leave? Why did you leave? Why did you leave? Why did you leave? Why does everyone keep leaving me? Why did you leave?

IV.

I know, I know. I'm being dramatic. I'm acting like I'm the victim. I do that sometimes, and I acknowledge it. It wasn't all bad, what you and I had. No, not at all. In fact, there was one point where you held onto *me* tightly, but I was too busy to realize how much you were hurting, and so you sought out people who looked at you, who understood you, who were there for you. And I tell myself that you left me, but that's not the case. Not really. It doesn't have to be; you found your people, that's all. The hardest thing I've had to do, I think, is acknowledge that I'm not perfect, either. Far from it, in fact. Now, after you've assisted me, shared my intensity, ignited it, even, caught a glimpse of who I was, truly, beyond my walls, I can find *my* people. It just happens—people move on. People change. We've changed. We're no longer best friends and haven't been for a long time, but that's a stupid term, anyway. A fake title used to make ourselves feel comforted, less alone in this big world. And that's fine. I'm glad you're happy now. I'm sorry I wasn't enough for you. I was never enough for you, was I?

It doesn't have to be this dramatic, Brittney. You feel things so intensely, like these feelings are permanent, like this emptiness is reality, like your phone, quiet, is the new norm. Everyone has highs and lows. Get over it. Stop thinking about it. Smile, it's okay. I promise, it'll be okay. You'll find a new friend in time, but for now, you have me.

Who are you?

I am you. I'll be here for you.

I won't be enough for you. You'll leave—they always leave.

Nope, no. We're not going there. Not today.
No more loose threads, okay?

I can't let go. Not yet.

V.

The rain trickles down the window and I smile because of course, as I'm writing this gloomy piece, it's raining. Perhaps this is a metaphor—I enjoy making connections in all things—for this moment, for this time in my life.

My 21st birthday is approaching and yet, I feel like my world has crumbled. Unsteady, uncertain, and new. Hollow in places, gray in others. And yet, there's hope because I've endured change before, change quite like this. It always gets better, always. With time and patience and self-awareness and self-compassion, good will come from this.

Flowers cannot sprout, cannot grow without the rain. April rain leads to May bloom. It's funny, when such a cliche turns out to have truth. I am all but a planted seed, buried under the wet earth, flooded with overwhelming emotion that is only nutrients for healing. Soon enough, the sun will emerge from beyond the clouds and I will flourish. Whatever that looks like, whatever happens, it'll be beautiful.

And then it'll happen again, over and over and over throughout my life.

People leave us, but we also leave them. We are always changing, morphing, growing, falling, being planted all over again. Nothing is permanent, nothing lasts forever.

Life wouldn't be nearly as interesting if everything stayed the same.

VI.

I stare at you from afar for a while. I see you smile as you confide in others, in your new circle, happy without me present, and my stomach twists with jealousy. An old friend, Jealousy. He always returns to screw with my head, even when I truly believe he has left for good.

In time, my hands heal, and my stomach untwists, and a familiar feeling floods into my chest, replacing the dense jealousy that paid a quick welcome—happiness. Oh, how I've missed you dearly. And not just happiness, but independence. Confidence. Love. *Relief.* The feeling of being enough for myself and myself alone.

See? I told you good would come from this. It feels nice here, where I am now. Light and airy.

I turn and walk away from you, descending into the unknown but feeling refreshed by the rain. I extend my fingers, stretch them, and reach out toward my reflection, looking at that girl in the mirror, in the eyes, for the first time in a long time.

I will never leave you, I whisper to myself.

And I never do.

Devoid of Expression

I am a trapped soul, a wandering mist. Perhaps even a figment of my own imagination. Or in simpler terms, I am a ghost.

My face does not exist and nor do my hands, nor my feet. My name is unknown and my thoughts retain no psychological meaning.

The people pass me by, their skin glowing, radiating life. Their eyes are vibrant colors as they scan their surroundings; mine remain gray and fixated on their diverse expressions. Some sip coffee, loosely grasping the cup, their intake of the liquid cautious despite their thirst for energy, for it is too hot to drink too quickly. Some bite into soft blueberry muffins, the aroma of them permeating the city. Some grip the hands of another, their gazes transfixed upon each other.

I stand within the crowds, my face devoid of expression. The people do not seem to notice me … they never have. Not once in 153 years. Of course, however, the occasional eyes darting my way when I stub my toe or knock over a stack of books is always somewhat enjoyable. I suppose it depends on the crowd. Nevertheless, I will forever remain invisible to all who roams the earth.

Why am I here? Now that is a good question, so good that I myself do not know the answer. In fact, I should've left a long time ago. A *very* long time ago. I do not remember what exactly occurred to trigger my death, but I remember flames snapping their flickering tails about the crisp, winter air. I remember the screams, the heat that crawled about my arms, my legs, boiling my skin and filling me with such intense agony that to this day, I still endure it. I have two scars to prove my memories: a subtle, jagged mark above my left collar bone, and a rather immense wound, wrinkled to the point that no normal skin is visible, stretching from my bicep to the center of my forearm, a long tendril extending to my wrist.

     I gaze upward to the towering buildings above, the windows glinting with the sun's vivid light. Boston wasn't always this way, evidently so, with structures less sturdy and not so extravagantly tall. And by what I've seen, nobody needs buildings so massive. But then again, suppose that given the resources of today's time, it'd be easy to continue growing. Matter of fact, people never tend to quit growing, changing… or discovering new ways to better themselves. Given the amount of time I've sat silently, watching the world develop, I've undoubtedly recognized such drastic changes, such growth.

     When I was alive, times were much different. My fogged awareness of my short-lived life brings me images of bricked pathways and ancient theatres … horses and carriages, newly founded companies. Now, all that remains are illuminated screens and eyes that seem oblivious to all that surrounds.

     Howbeit, I am not oblivious like the rest, for my resources are limited. I see all, for what else is there to do as a ghost? I enjoy creeping into homes at night and trading my conscious thoughts for a wildly unique story, the dusted covers of the books clamped tightly within my weak grasp, made up of bony, pale knuckles. Moreover, I also luxuriate in attending musicals, as well as wandering about art museums, my eyes scanning the polished dancers and walls coated in splattered paint. Luckily, I am stuck in a city with much to do … I never thought I'd say the word 'stuck' in a positive remark.

    Currently, I saunter about the streets, nothing but a cold chill felt as I emerge into the crowds, brushing past with thin fingers. I clutch the sides of my frock coat -- usually left undone and down at my sides -- tugging it downwards, feeling the black fabric between the tips of my fingers. My gray cloth trousers fit loosely around my legs, my white cloth shirt untucked and blanketed by a coat of blackened smoke. You'd think such a stain would be absent by now, but perhaps I'm mistaken. My leather shoes *clonk* against the cement sidewalk… such a pity that I am the only one aware of their sound.

    This is all that I own.

    At one point, I was insane. Of course, who, in my position, wouldn't be? Silence does that to you, I suppose. And being alone is quite annoying, especially when you cannot do anything about it. Nobody can hear me, feel me, see me… I live alone among an overpopulated world.

    I've been present for every event of Boston since 1863. I've watched the people migrate west, while I've remained trapped behind an invisible wall. I've listened to the anti-slavery speeches; I've seen the Irish flood in from across the ocean. I was there when the Boston Red Sox (formerly known as the Boston Pilgrims) won the world series. I sat and watched The Great Molasses Flood kill the innocent.

Kill. Death. Such odd words. Is there even such a thing as an afterlife? I've read every novel on such word… religion, Heaven and Hell, souls. Ghosts. I wonder to myself if there are trapped souls like me, wandering the Earth, with nobody to converse with except for their crazed minds.

When I was insane, I'd try to end this strange, in-between phase I am forever trapped in. I'd run a knife through my skin, but no blood would flow. I'd leap into the Charles River, holding my nose and waiting anxiously for my lungs to collapse… but they never did. I've fallen from the Prudential Tower countless times, landing perfectly on my leather shoes no matter how forcefully I fell.

So, I've stopped trying … not only because I literally cannot take my life and at last, lie to rest, but perhaps because subconsciously I still believe my life acquires a purpose. Because I am immortal, somewhere inside I find myself clinging to some form of hope, pulling it towards myself, my skin tearing and burning, but never letting go.

But then again, perhaps this is all just self reassurance, and the real reason I haven't gone entirely mad is because of Callie Kline. Though I'd hate to admit this to myself; it would propose that I am absent of worth. But, who am I kidding, I'm a ghost.

Abruptly, my neck jolts up, my posture straightening. Warmth bundles me up as I see her now, striding toward an office building, just two blocks from her apartment. She drinks her coffee steadily, as though she's sampling it, determining whether she savors the flavor. Her soft, rose-colored lips kiss the lid, her tongue wiping them clean as she pulls away. She's a coffee addict, and I'm afraid it's terrifically obvious to even a stranger. Her deep brown eyes are wide and observant, her slender fingers tapping the side of the cup.

She wears a worn pencil behind her left ear, her shoulder-length, sandy brown hair blow-dried and slightly draped over her high-set cheekbones. Her figure is shapely, her black slacks fitting her neatly and a maroon blouse tucked in, flowing with the gentle breeze.

Callie Anne Kline. Even her name sends a shiver down my spine; she's gorgeous… magnificent.

She brushes past me, with no clue that I am standing so near to her. No care, either. And she carries on, crossing the street, just sipping her coffee.

No matter how many 26-year-old women there are thriving in Boston, she's the only one I've noticed, ever. She's the only one that I've imagined kissing sweetly … imagined feeling the natural softness of her fingertips as she strokes my neck. The only one I've imagined looking into my eyes and *seeing* me, *understanding* me.

"Stop that," Benjamin snaps to me. "It's useless … pointless … she's never going to see you." Benjamin is my mind, and frankly, he is rather frustrating.

"I don't care," I murmur in reply, stuffing my hands into my pockets, watching Callie's kitten heels *click clack* across the street. "There's just something about her... something about the way she moves, the way she talks. I can't describe it, Benjamin." The chilled air catches my soft voice, carrying it further from me until it is once again nonexistent.

"Suit yourself," my mind sighs.

I've been watching Callie Kline for four years. Well, watching sounds as though I am a freak, or a stalker. But then again, I suppose I am.

Is it odd that I've been practicing what to say to her this entire time? Maybe, maybe not. But perhaps one day, one miraculous day, she'll see me and we'll talk for hours. I mean, we'd *have* too... but would we even get along? I'd like to think that we would; everything she says is remarkable. Brilliant, even. She comes up with ideas that I never even knew existed, and each word she speaks leaves me breathless for more.

She's the most intelligent person I know. However, I don't feel that she agrees.

Callie Kline works in an office building with gray walls and stained carpet, and undoubtedly she thrives to be more. An aspiring author, to be specific: each night after answering sales calls and gnawing on her pen, she comes home to her cramped, one-bedroom apartment, a steamy cup of coffee -- flavored with one packet of sweetener and two tablespoons of cream -- between her palms, and a laptop placed before her, the glowing blue light of a Word Document shadowing the holes beneath her eyes. And she writes ... and writes and writes and writes, her ideas exploding from her vast mind like a volcano demanding to be emptied.

I enjoy concentrating on Callie's face as she writes -- she furrows her eyebrows and mouths the words she intends to type. I usually stand near, but not too near, so that she can be as alone as possible … so that she can be set free.

Her stories are glorious, but she continues to start over. She never finishes. Never shows anyone her work, for she is afraid. So many times I have sat close to her, my gaze glued to hers. "Quit starting over," I whisper to her. "Take a chance."

However, she doesn't listen.

As cliche as it is, Callie makes me feel alive; it's as though my heart leaps, my lungs expand … as though a warmth itches across the back of my neck. I've experienced feelings like these before, in 1860 … I vaguely remember caressing a bare shoulder of another woman. However, I do not remember the feelings I endure now, with Callie; all I remember from those images are filthy clouds of lust and meaningless pleasure.

My attention regains focus on the present, and I follow Callie Kline into her office building. The ceilings are tall, the voices echoing about the space, and I glide past the living. They wear slacks similar to Callie's… clean and shimmering with the light of the chandeliers. I gaze toward a glass wall as I pass it, my eyes scanning over my appearance. It's quite humorous actually: I've looked the same since 1863, when I was about 28, I believe. Maybe 30. Maybe even 22. But I'll admit, part of me always expects to see something different. Perhaps my hair will become blonde instead of murky brown. Perhaps my skin won't be as pale.

And perhaps, even, I won't be dead.

"You are a ghost," Benjamin informs me as my thoughts once again take the better of me. "You are nonexistent. You are nothing."

"Thanks for reminding me," I reply bluntly, my thin, white lips pressed into a line.

"Just saying."

Callie enters an elevator. She is alone, her eyes staring toward the coral-colored walls as the doors begin to close. But, before they do, I join her.

"Hey Callie," I say to her, a warm smirk spreading across my face.

She doesn't reply, but I imagine she does. A smile warily emerges onto my emancipated face, my eyes transfixed upon her distant stare.

"She can't see you," my mind mumbles.

"Silence, Benjamin!" I holler.

The doors of the elevator begin to open, and Callie flicks her hair over her right shoulder before continuing toward her office.

She smiles kindly to the receptionist, then to Marcus. I despise Marcus, with his clean-cut black hair and broad frame. Of course, I could respond to his flirtations with Callie by becoming a stereotypical ghost, flickering his lights on and off and tossing knives across his kitchen. But then again, that would be rather rude.

Nevertheless, he's a complete fool.

I sit with Callie most of the day, engaging in casual conversation with her. She works most of the time, but plays a game titled Poptropica when her manager cannot see. I chuckle when she does this, leaning back against the wall and stretching my arms.

It's humorous how times have changed so dramatically, yet stay so similar: people continue to lie and cheat … but they also continue to play. They continue to experience and make the most out of life, for life is brief and unexpected, and perhaps even unjust.

Once in a while, however, injustice becomes the most wondrous occurrence.

I've known Callie Kline since she was 22, when she first arrived in Boston. She was young, fresh out of college with nothing but a three-year-old Persian cat and a Liberal Arts degree. To this day, I can still visualize the moment my eyes spotted her in the crowd. She bit her lip, her bright eyes frantic as they flickered about the crowded streets of Boston. She watched the taxi cabs speed by, the extravagant lights blanketing her skin. I approached her gently, my head bowing slightly, my lips parting in awe.

I had never seen such a beautiful human being in all of my existence.

And from then on, I remained at her side. I've watched her meticulous movements as she paints strokes of blue upon blank canvases. I've watched her fall in love, I've watched her heart shatter. I've watched her tell stories of magic and mystery and love. I've watched her create.

I joined Callie on a date a couple years back. I strolled with her to an Italian restaurant, admiring her slimming green dress and gold jewels. And once her and the man -- his name, I remember, was Evan -- were seated at the candle-lit table, I observed them both from a distance. My arms were crossed and my lips were pursed as I watched Callie laugh with that strange man named Evan, whose attire was much too neat, his appearance handsome and well-groomed.

Evan couldn't quit blushing like a child on their birthday, which sent waves of heated agitation through myself. Frankly, moments are never awkward with Callie; no matter how odd or dull the conversation, she responds with a glittering smile and a kind reply. Every man adores her for this. Or, at least I do… and Evan *did*.

After the date, when Callie returned to her apartment, she yanked off her dress—I promise I closed my eyes like any gentleman would—and slipped into cloth pajama shorts and a stained t-shirt. She turned on the television, leaning back into her sofa, her cat curled up in her lap. She must've sat there for hours, all throughout the night, watching house-renovation shows. And whenever the couples were first introduced, she would stroke her cat and whisper, "One day, I will find a man, and I will love him. And I will be happy."

If only she knew how close I was to her during that moment.

For the duration of those four years, not once has the thought of me crossed her mind. Of course, I've considered that perhaps, even if I were alive, she still wouldn't think of me. Why would her mind, being as vast as it is, care about a pale, awestruck man dressed in dirty clothing very much out-of-date?

I think back to my purpose. If a God exists, why didn't he take me? I do not recall ever doing such harm, such bad. I was only 22, maybe 30… surely, I couldn't have been so horrific as to receive such punishment.

I remember emerging from the depths of the Charles River after nearly an hour of hoping for my final death, everlasting slumber, hollering curses to the sky, tears boiling within my eyes.

These thoughts bring a frown to settle on my face as I wonder: I don't know if I can endure another day of being invisible to Callie. Of wondering how she'd react if she knew how I felt. Of wondering how she'd react if I told her how perfect she is to me… how wonderful.

Callie Kline gives my life meaning. But she's also slowly destroying it, or at least whatever remains of it. Is my life technically even considered a life? I mean, I am dead. A wandering mist.

Perhaps even a figment of my own imagination.

At six o'clock, Callie leaves the office, and I follow her as she says her farewells to her coworkers, descends the elevator, and hastily strolls out the front doors without another word, her lips sealed.

Outside, the sun is setting, the chilled air breathing against us both. The streetlights blink on, the taxi cabs honking, people scattered about the sidewalks, some smoking a cigarette, some begging for money.

Tonight, however, Callie Kline does not turn onto her street. I gaze at her carefully, wondering if she is okay, wondering what she could be thinking about. She crosses her arms, her eyes dewy as she saunters toward Central Park. I float alongside her, my gray eyes curious and somewhat frightful: Callie Kline has never done this before.

    We approach the park, and it is now nearly seven at night. The stars begin to appear, glittering. It is funny, that for 153 years, the stars have remained in the same positions, and the moon is just as bright as it once was before I died.

    I died at night; I vaguely remember the darkness consuming me whole as my eyes forced themselves shut and my body settled into a stiffness.

    I vaguely remember reaching toward the hand of another, burned raw from the flames, as heat nipped at my calves, my forearms. Or, in other words, I died saving someone from a fire. Or, at least trying to. So, why did I end up here, stuck and trapped… as a lost soul? Disparagingly, I understand that such depressing thoughts will not help me, nor revive me… but a human being cannot help but question, even when they no longer exist.

    Callie Kline seats herself on a park bench, bowing her head, gazing forward at the Charles River. Her stare is solemn, yet her mind is loud; I can hear her thoughts erupting into madness. I seat myself beside her, observing her face, which to me, is as a wishing well… deep and mysterious, full of wonders beyond my knowledge. Her mind beholds such treasures that even I dare grasp.

    All my lonesome life, I have never met someone so beautiful, so pure. So intelligent. Her eyes, so clear-sighted and filled with such intensity, brings myself to consider whether or not she is like me… like me being that she is a ghost herself, a lost soul, absent of any idea of where to go, where to venture to next. She's stuck in one spot, with unrealistic dreams and too many questions to answer.

My thoughts are interrupted when she raises her chin, and begins to speak in a voice as gentle as the rippling waves of water, "Why am I so alone? Is this my fate, my destiny? Is it not my purpose to be successful with my writing? For goodness sake, I am 26-years-old with no prospects, no boyfriend, no family, no money… why am I so *alone*?" Tears begin to pour down her cheeks, past her lips, dripping from her chin. She wipes them away with a shaky hand. "I have always wanted to be so much more, so why can't I? Why can't someone love me? Why can't I excel in my talents? Why am I stuck here, in Boston? Why can't I escape?"

My eyes widen, her sudden sadness engrossing me more than anything ever has. I would've never imagined Callie Kline to be so sorrowful, so melancholy.

"You have me, Callie Kline," I speak to her gently. "I've always been here … trust me. I, myself, am stuck, too. We can achieve anything together… I promise."

As expected, Callie Kline does not respond. Instead, she sniffles, her thumbs fidgeting in her lap, her hair gently blown back by the current breeze.

Beneath the darkness, I see her eyes glisten, reflecting the moonlight. I see her lips part gently, wet from the tears. I see her face. I see her mind.

I see *her*.

"I am so in love with you," I breathe out.

And then, ever so gently, her head tilts, her eyes augment, her pupils dramatically enlarge, and her breath hastens. She cautiously turns her head, her frantic gaze suddenly finding mine. And amidst the night, beyond the noisy streets, the busy, oblivious people, the altering world … we stare at each other.

And she sees me.

Transformation

Laughter.

Shrieks of joy.

The songs of happiness trail my apartment, late at night, like dense smoke. It fills my lungs. I can't breathe.

Why wasn't I invited?

I'm lying in bed, the sheets pulled up to my chin, and my body is still, like a wooden plank. My eyes are wide, boring into the ceiling above my head. My cat is curled up at my side, purring. At least I have her.

Even so, I can't sleep. No.

Right now, I can't stop imagining everything seemingly wrong with me. In fact, I am taken back to an image, vivid and haunting, still.

I am a child, maybe eight, or nine, curled up behind a trash can while the rest of the children are playing, and I'm writing furiously into a journal. It's a story, one of several, that homes my mind. This one in particular is about snow leopards, their bonds, and their treacherous journeys through the snow.

A group of girls walks toward me, grinning down, fire dancing in their eyes.

One of them asks me, sneering, "What are you doing?"

I glance up at them. "Writing a book." My voice is sheepish, soft.

They snicker. "Yeah, *right*."

"I'm not lying."

"Well, then I bet it's a pretty bad book."

It's the next day. The laughs have stopped, yet the voices in my own imagination have not. My mind, shadowed with falsities and darkened realities, yearns for a distraction.

I turn on a YouTube video, and I start dancing.

Now, I haven't moved my body in quite some time. Ten minutes in and I'm on the floor, breathing heavily, my legs two wooden sticks and my abs tight as a rock.

The next day, I turn on a video as well, and I dance again. Longer this time.

A week later, I incorporate weights. Thirty minutes a day, every day. That is my new goal.

It's helping—the voices are dissipating, shrinking to the back of my consciousness and retaining less weight, less importance.

But the laughs, those continue. I walk through the doors of my home, and am hardly looked at, barely acknowledged. Tonight is game night. What fun. In my bedroom, I turn on my daily video, and move. I imagine that with each harsh breath I'm pushing out the loneliness, the fears, the darkness of my mind that rages. The purple, murky depths.

The memories are still here. They seem to always find me. At a birthday party. A pool party, specifically. The girls, they comment on how large my thighs are, on how freakishly tall I am compared to them. I laugh with them because at that time, I thought such comments were funny, even though they hurt. We all take photos together, smiles wide and ecstatic, seemingly innocent.

I am cut out of every single photo. I'm not even tagged when they're posted online.

It's like I don't even exist. Sometimes, I wonder if anyone can even see me at all.

If anyone even knows my name.

The workout videos transition to running—there's not much to do these days, now that everyone is stuck inside.

And, well, my own home is terribly unwelcoming.

I strap on my shoes and go and pretend that I'm flying through the morning air, dense and chilly on my skin. I imagine that I am running from everything and everyone who has ever hurt me or ignored me or used me or picked on me or pretended as though I didn't have any feelings at all or called me strange or not good enough and I'm running faster now, darting down the street, tears streaming down my face because I'm doing it. Yes, I'm doing it.

I'm *healing*.

And I'm doing it on my own.

But the memories, they don't stop.

I'm in class, and a girl turns to me and whispers, "She's only friends with you because she's forced to by her mom."

I'm in the hallway when a girl says to me, "A little birdie told me that you're a terrible person."

I'm in the car when my old friend throws a penny at my head, hard.

I'm in bed when he walks into my room, and I lie, so still, until he's done.

I'm in a coffee shop when my best friend tells me that I'm selfish and fake and everyone in my life has been secretly talking about me behind my back and none of my friends actually like me.

I'm on the bleachers when my boyfriend tells me he doesn't love me anymore.

I'm at home when I confront my friend about not inviting me to her Christmas party and she says, "You're like an annoying little puppy."

I'm at prom, dressed like Belle in a golden, glimmering dress that fit like a gown with statements of simple, gold jewelry, when my boyfriend ignores me for the entirety of the night and flirts with my best friend instead. Later that night, at home, I'm dumped by him.

I'm in class when a teacher picks up my bullet journal and hurls it across the classroom. Oh, that same teacher? He told me that my published book wasn't that impressive and proceeded to call me a "show-off" in front of everyone. And everyone laughed.

For the remainder of the school year, this teacher picks on me like I'm a helpless child, as though it gives him pleasure.

It probably did.

I'm outside, and I'm still running.

They move out of the apartment, I even help them move, because I'm me, and it is calm now. I take a trip to a craft store and choose items to redecorate, make the space feel more like mine. I even light some incense burn a little sage. There's a new energy to this place. Happy. Safe. A few months pass, and I welcome new, kinder souls into this home, that is mine as equally as it is there's.

I no longer hide in my room. No. I bathe in this newfound sense of welcoming.

I'm eight, or nine, and I've finished my snow leopard story. My teacher peers over my shoulder, noticing it, and asks me what it is. And I hesitate, tell her softly, "It's a book."

"Is that so? That is so neat. May I read it?" she asks me, evidently intrigued.

I nod, hand it to her. She carries it back to her desk, proceeding to read the sixty pages of sloppy, horribly misspelled writing. I eye her as she flips through the pages, my heart in my throat.

At the end of the day, she returns, hands it back to me and says, "This is really, *really* good Brittney. You're going to be an excellent writer one day. In fact, you already are an excellent writer. Keep writing, okay?"

The mean girls stare at her as she says this, almost as though they are confused.

It's night, but I find that I'm no longer scared of the dark. Of being alone. Laughs trail the hallways, but they don't affect me. Not like they used to.

A candle is flickering a gentle flame. My overhead string lights create a comfortable ambiance. I'm lying on the floor, listening to the sound of my overhead fan, whirring. A cup of chamomile tea wafts warm stream to the right of me.

I'm home. Physically, and mentally. I am present in my skin.

I no longer pity myself. No. I have recognized the fact that everyone has been through depths, through pain. But from that, we heal. Grow.

We cannot transform unless we have the motivation to do so.

So, thank you. Thank you, mean girls, thank you, old boyfriends, thank you to the teachers who didn't believe in me, and thank you to the teachers who did. Because without you, any of you, I highly doubt I'd have anything worth writing about.

I have good memories, too.

I'm in class, laughing hysterically with my friends in English, my favorite part of the day, our faces bright red, smiles so wide, it's like they were drew on.

I'm in the car when I take a spontaneous trip with a friend to buy myself some fish.

I'm in bed with the love of my life, and he wraps his arms around me, tight, and I melt into him, as though I have always belonged encased in his skin.

I'm in a coffee shop with a friend and we're writing our books together, headphones on, coffee now cold, eyes focused on our laptop screens.

I'm on the bleachers after completing my first race in a swim meet, the 100 freestyle, and I'm panting and I'm watching my friends and cheering them on, my stomach knotted with nerves that always come with swim meets.

I'm at home, with my family, settled in the living room on a Wednesday night, a school night, watching reality television before bed, and a cat is purring softly in my lap.

I'm at homecoming with a group of friends from my AP Physics 2 class and we're dancing, pretty badly, to the crappy music that blares. I'm even asked to dance, and he chooses a song I briefly mentioned I liked months prior.
Later that night, I smile, feeling endlessly lucky.
I'm in class, when the high school principal calls me to the hallway, and terrified, I follow. She sits me down in the library and proceeds to tell me that she just finished my first novel and is blown away but how good it is, written by someone as young as I.
For the remainder of the year, she beams at me in the hallways, sometimes even asks if I'm working on anything new.
I'm outside, and I'm still running. Farther, and farther still, and with this continuous running blossoms a newfound love of feeling my body slice through the air, of feeling my feet slam against the pavement, of being fully immersed in my skin, in my mind. Of feeling glad, proud, to be *me*. At this moment, a year later, I am forty pounds lighter, which I presume was weight I had stored for these exact moments, to fuel the fight to find my worth. My body is entirely different now, so different that it doesn't always feel like my own. But it is—I know it is. Because this body, this mind, what's remaining of both, is the true version of myself—unafraid, stronger than any voice or memory or haunting—which had really been there all along, deep beneath the falsities.
Now, all that lies ahead is endless room to grow, and space to hang my race medals. Oh, how there is so much more beauty ahead. I can hardly believe it.

How much I've transformed.

I am hugging myself, my younger self, who is eight, or nine, and I'm holding her tight. So, very tight. My tears soak her shirt as I pull her toward me, closer. And I tell her, "Keep fighting, little me. Please, don't let them get to you. Don't let any one of them make you think that you're an ounce less than what you are—a magical, creative, strong, beautiful girl. I love you. Never forget that. You hear me? I *love* you." The tears fall harder now, but they're not sad tears, no. They're happy tears, because I didn't stop fighting—I never stopped, for *her*, that little version of me. "You can do it. Just wait. The life just ahead of you will be absolutely wonderful."

And it is.

The Colors of Me, of You, of Us

Red.

  Boiling, bubbling, rising heat, swelled in my gut, trapped in my throat, hot fiery breath, panting, sweet to the taste, stinging, trembling perfidiously, my fists at my sides, squeezed, hard. Beads of sweat, sticky on my skin, eyes, narrowed, tears, begging to press forward but no, no, not now. My heart, it pounds at the base of my throat, and I just want to dive into your skin, become a part of you, until death do us part, but I can't give in, no, no, not yet. The world, it blurs, a watercolor painting around me, and all I can see is red. The red, it surrounds me, demands to be unleashed, demands to be heard, passionate and angry all at once but I'm stronger, at least for a while longer. My fists, squeezed tighter, the heat, it rises still, my chest tight, knotted, my breath quick, shallow, I hold so still, containing it, and you speak, your tone harsh, a bit defensive, but not rude, but it doesn't matter. You tell me you love me. You tell me you hate me. The red, it expands, and the heat, it rises, pours out of me, and I feel myself tipping, falling. It will take me quite a while to stand back up. To calm myself. To slow… down.

  To fix what I have done.

  It subsides, it always does, the red softening, blending, descending, and then the day is over, the sunset fading out of view.

Orange.

The color of the sunrise and the color of you, your lopsided smile, your crazy hair. The color of your music, pop but jazz and there's a beat to it, the kind of beat you want to dance to, you want to bop your head to, you want to smile to. You, you have a kind of beat to you, and you want to smile, you just do, when you're around you. First thing in the morning, as the sunlight trickles in, your music plays sweet orange to my ears, blossoming, unfolding the day to come. You rise, put on your glasses and beam down at me, offer to make me coffee, offer to do absolutely anything because you know I'm still tired and absolutely despise getting out of bed this early. Your smile remains, always, all day it seems, radiating warmth, softness, and I could curl right up into you, you and your orange light, your quirky dances and hysterical laugh and your never-ending creativity, the bellow of the trumpet from the hall, the unmade bed, the hipster clothing and hipster decorations and hipster everything, buying a glass jar of milk just because it looks cool, all of the joy you bring. The sun is setting over the horizon and we're in the car, driving somewhere, and you're grinning at me like a fool, just admiring me. You make me feel so special. Orange popsicles on a summer day, sipping homemade moscow mules, your hand clammy in mine, and we're laughing about something you said.

Yellow.

A different summer day. I am walking in the afternoon and I see the sunlight glinting off the swaying grass and it is lovely. The warmth caresses my skin, and

I'm grinning for no reason at all, other than the fact that I am happy. Happy to be here, on this walk, the breeze cool on my skin, shimmering with sweat, by myself but not afraid, for the first time in a while, to be by myself. Yellow, a happy color, the color of purity, of warmth, of new beginnings, of the sun, and all of it's light. Is there more to be said? Cozy mornings, sipping coffee, watching the sunrays dance above my head, pieces of dust floating. The glow at the end of a long, dark tunnel, pulling me forward, and I race into it, into the yellow. I am embraced by it, enveloped in the cheery feeling of being alive, of being on a walk, and admiring the world. Of being, once again, whole. Of feeling airy, light, and free. Endlessly free.

Green.

     Sometimes, freedom can be daunting, unknown, the path stretched out before me, the ending out of sight. In these cases, I return to the Earth, of course. The trees, they whisper to me. Come here, we'll tell you our secrets, we'll teach you how to be still. So, still. I am lying on the grass and feeling Her hum beneath me, the roots dancing, reaching, growing. I am immersed in nature, and I wish I always was. There are trees outside of my apartment and sometimes, when I lie in bed a certain way, the trees are all that I can see, and I pretend that I am surrounded by trees, encased in a forest, far, far away, and safe, and quiet. There are no sounds besides the sway of the trees, their whispers. The blossoming flowers, the abundance of produce, skin speckled with dew, fresh, morning air, dense in my lungs. When the world is chaotic, internally, externally, I return to nature, to the ground, stable and secure beneath my feet. My palms rest on my stomach as I breathe in, breathe out, calm.

If I could give myself a color, it would be green. Forest green, Earthy green, grounded green. One with nature and all that it is. Sometimes I wish I could meld into the ground and become all but a root. I would watch the leaves rustle above my head, listen to the sweet sounds of the natural world, and descend, down, deep down, deeper, and deeper, until I am the Earth.

Until I am home.

Blue.

In bed, the pillow soft beneath my head, feeling nothing, only melancholia, but in a relaxed, comforted sort of way. The ocean, the waves, the deep, vast blue beneath me, the rain pouring outside my window, the record player turning, humming classical music softly in the background, the gentle piano riffs and melodramatic strings, the river that flows, your tears soaking my shirt, I pull you closer toward me, absorbing your blue. Sadness that cannot be described, only felt, deeply. Loneliness that swells, consumes, until it is difficult to exhale comfortably. An emptiness that expands, leaving you hollow. But, calm, and you can't explain it. It's like you're floating, drifting away on this ocean, staring up into the bright, blue sky, riding the waves that carry you, rising and falling. You're just feeling blue today, and that's okay. Your cat leaps onto the bed, curls up beside you, and you hold her tight, and in time, you sob all over her fur. But she doesn't move. No, she stays, absorbing your blue.

In time, you will rise, but not now. No, not now. Now, it is time to rest. Maybe brew some tea. Do some light stretches. Perhaps sink even deeper. Sometimes, it feels nice to be fully and entirely submerged beneath the ocean, drowning in the feelings that crowd your mind. Sometimes, it feels nicer than feeling nothing, empty, melancholy. But sometimes, feeling nothing feels good, too.

The rain, it continues to patter on my window, and I watch it from my bed, curling into my messy bed sheets, my tears drying under my eyes.

Purple.

The sky darkens now, a deep blue transitioning into an eerie purple that settles, hanging over us, a haunting reminder of the storm that is brewing, that will be here soon. The sky, dark but brought forth by the glimmer of bold, purple light that outlines the clouds, which have quickened in pace. Lightning slashes, the thunder follows, shaking my bedroom.

Purple is what I felt when I lost you. Sitting on the steps, staring aimlessly into the wall, into the abyss, trying to make sense of myself, of what has happened, of what I should do now, moving forward. So low. Lower than ever before. Thick sludge, murky depths, dark, oh, so dark, sticky tar clogs my throat, my chest, and I can't breathe. I am lying on the floor, staring up at the ceiling, and it is worse than blue because I am not calm, no, I am deep.

Too deep. Too far in my head. Trapped, overwhelming emotions flooding my mind, the weight of myself so heavy, I can't lift my arms, I can't open my eyes, nor close them. I am just existing in this space, with this purple. My old friends, they'd confide in me about anything and everything, and I'd leave, sticky with purple that'd only come off after a long shower, a good cry. I search the news for hours, taking in all that I read, and the purple reappears, clings to me. Deep, dense purple. My worst enemy. My worst fears.

    I'm so still, but I am here. Yes, I am still here.

    Sometimes, purple can be good. Purple shows you who you truly are, brings everything forth, and you are forced to face it, face yourself, face the voices, the whispers, that call to you. Night drives, "Crybaby" by Kevin Morby or "Wildflower" by Beach House or something else ethereal and euphoric blasting from my car radio, the light guides me down the dark road, the feelings rise, encasing me in a comforting cloak, a deep embrace, and I inhale a shaky breath, manage to smile, through it all.

    I am still here.

The Tale of the Hummingbird

There is a tale of a hummingbird who wanted to be a part of everything. She wanted to drink the nectar of every flower, wanted to befriend every animal in the forest, even the mice, even the beetles, and she also wanted to be everything; she wanted to be the mice, be the beetles, even the humans, who she observed from a distance and found quite fascinating, indeed. Most of all, however, she wanted to be a jackhammer. She admired the way they pecked at the tree, endlessly, with one goal in mind. They never minded being jackhammers, and never did they wish they were someone else, a part of something larger than themselves. All they cared about was catching that worm, plump and wriggling frantically before being swallowed for lunch. Then, onto the next tree they went, and to the next, endlessly and without fail nor boredom.

The hummingbird was always bored. Well, not always, but most of the time. Nothing was quite enough for her, hence the reason she always wanted to be part of something else. A single flower was only temporary alleviation, a band aid for her boredom, and so she'd travel, her wings fluttering vigorously throughout the forest, searching for the *next* perfect one. She'd find it, soon enough, slurp up it's sweetness, feeling full and satisfied, but only momentarily. You see, the nectar was only fleeting happiness to her, fleeting, and she never understood how the mice or the beetles or the jackhammers or the people could be so perfectly satisfied with their lives. Why was she always searching for more? Why was being just… *her*, never enough?

To fulfill her need for happiness, she'd flutter down to the forest floor and mingle with the mice. With a sideways glance and no response, they'd scurry off. She'd even plop down on the floor, scurry alongside them. I'm just like you, she'd say. I'm just being a mouse for the day, and still, they wouldn't even glance her way, mindlessly sniffing around for their afternoon snack.

She'd visit the beetles that crawled at the bases of the trees, and they, unlike the mice, would acknowledge her, yet barely. You can't be a beetle, they'd inform her. You are a hummingbird. When she told them that anything is possible if you believe it is, they chuckled, then crawled back down into their little cave in the dirt.

The jackhammers were the kindest of all the forest animals. In fact, they taught her how to keep her mind sharp and focused on one goal: finding food. They welcomed her under their wings, told her that she didn't need to be a mouse or a beetle to be happy. She didn't have to be anyone but herself. True happiness meant following your goals, choosing one path, accepting yourself as you are, and working hard. For a while, she believed them, followed this way of life herself, and rather than trying to be anyone she wasn't, she spent her days looking for nectar, slurping it up, and repeating, endlessly, just like the jackhammers. When the temporary happiness had faded, she'd scout out another flower, and another, replacing the blossoming feeling that'd appear, fill her with brightness, then dissipate.

However, this was the problem she hadn't realized: while she was being a hummingbird, she was still following the ways of the jackhammers. She was still terribly bored and the longing for a purpose swelled deeply inside of her. Still, even after having a single goal, learning to accept her path… she was deeply unhappy.

One day, she left the jackhammers to be by herself when she ran into a pack of hummingbirds. In fact, she hadn't seen any in quite some time; she had traveled far from her home to find herself. When they saw her, they swarmed her with joy and love. And yet, as thrilled as she was to see them, she felt even more sad, a pit of emptiness filling her chest. What is wrong? A brightly yellow hummingbird with a black beak asked. And so, she told them, honestly, what she had been feeling; lost, purposeless, unhappy, having trouble finding her identity, and so on. It was quite embarrassing for her to admit this, but she managed through and bowed her head, waited for them to laugh and carry on.

Instead, a red hummingbird drew in closer, it's wings creating wisps of cool breeze around them, and he told her, Why, you already have a purpose, sister. You are a hummingbird.

I want to be more than a hummingbird, she cried. I want to be a mouse and a beetle and a jackhammer and a human, I don't want to just fly around, drinking nectar, endlessly. How can you be okay with living this life, forever?

Do you know what it means to be a hummingbird? He asked.

Yes, we drink nectar and fly.

When you drink the nectar, dear sister, you are pollinating the plants and the flowers, and you are giving life to the mice and the beetles and the jackhammers and the people and to this forest as a whole. The beauty of being a hummingbird is that you aren't just a creature in the forest, looking for food, but you are already a part of everything, trailing the forest with sweet nectar to assist in all living things.

She paused for a moment, allowing this knowledge to sink in. Then, she asked, So why am I still unhappy?

Because you are trying to be someone you're not. You are trying to fit into the right life, be the right creature, find the perfect path. But, there is no "right" nor "perfect". Being a hummingbird, you are destined to live a colorful, ever-changing life. You are not happy because you are not out there, living a colorful life, but are forcing a life you think you should be living. You already *are* everything, sister, if that is what you desire.

She blinked at the red hummingbird, then nodded. You are right, brother. Why have I never thought of this before?

Come with us, he said. Let's pollinate the world.

And so, she followed, wings fluttering in unison, bright and bold and ever-changing against the green of the forest, without a goal or purpose and yet, remaining the most vibrant creature, giving life to each corner and crevice.

The funny thing is, when she stopped trying to be someone, she finally found herself, a creature of many purposes, many interests, without one path, one direction to follow, but an endless array of paths, journeys. Vibrant, creative, flying backwards, and forwards, simply, at rest, simply, a hummingbird.

Afterword

How does it feel, to have glimpsed inside my mind? Perhaps, inside your own? I hope you feel… understood.

For a while, I debated between writing an afterword. It almost felt as though something was missing, and yet, I felt like I had already said enough. More than enough. How do I correctly end this? When is something finished?

Do you know that feeling? When you've just wrapped up a wonderful conversation with a dear friend, in which y'all dove deep into each other's turmoil, emotions, and secrets, and although the conversation has clearly ended, it feels incomplete? Like an open wound left slit and raw to the earth? That feeling, almost a stubbornness, that overcomes both of you, an incompleteness. How do we end this vulnerable conversation so that we don't return to our homes, damaged, cut open like a piece of fruit, leaking out all over the place?

I came across one more piece. Well, specifically something I had written to be posted on my blog when I was a freshman in college. I am a senior now, preparing for graduation, dorm life, and all the memories that came with it, only a vague memory from a mind that has long sense changed, morphed—oh, how time flies! I uploaded the piece, then quickly decided against it, decided such a piece was too raw for the public, and removed it from all eyes. However, stumbling into it, years later, tears pooled around me, and so badly I wished to reach out, hold the me that wrote this piece three years prior and assure her that she would get through it, whatever she was going through. The amount of growth I've endured is immense, and I believe that after reading these pieces, there needs to be some sort of silent closure—an evident representation of the winding path I've traveled throughout my college years, contrasted with where I once was, standing at the start of it all. I believe that in this piece, I unknowingly composed the perfect afterword, the best ending of this conversation, or at least, better than anything I could have pried out of my brain that is now mush and unbearably naked to the world. So, this piece… well, it is how I will end this. How I will return to my comfortable bubble, and you, yours, and we can zip of those wounds, correctly.

First, let's raise our glasses in an imaginary cheers, to the girl I once was, the person all of us once were, and the people we are now, and the people we will be, in time. Let's cheers to this wonderful, little life of our known.

Without further ado, I present to you, "Welcome to the Mind of a College Freshman", preserved as it was first written in December of 2018..

Welcome to the Mind of a College Freshman

I wake up and it is early. My eyes flutter open, my mind foggy from last night's abnormally vivid dream--the images linger for a while, and I aimlessly collect them as I continue lying in bed. I think about this new day, curling tighter into my warm comforters and smacking my chapped lips. I can see myself in the full-length mirror from where I lie, and so I smile at myself.

After about thirty minutes of thinking, I rise from the lofted bed and hop down onto the chilled floor and for a few moments, I pace around in circles for the room is small and I am in desperate need of movement. My arms reach over my head and my back pops softly and my neck pops violently and I feel that all of my carried tension has been released.

Time for coffee. Goodness, I can already *smell* it-- the aroma fills the air and only a few everlasting moments after turning on the Keurig, it is ready. I lift the cup to my lips, sipping gently, letting every sense wander in my mind for a while. I do this because for some strange reason, this thick, brown, creamy liquid feels like home to me--one of the few things I have to remind me of the life I used to have.

After coffee, I brush my teeth and look myself sternly in the eyes. My hair is a mess, matted in odd places and sticking straight up in the back like a lion's mane.

When I finish brushing my teeth, I flash a smile, fix up my hair a bit, remind myself that I am me.

Now, I won't go into too much detail concerning my morning, because all mornings are relatively the same. Let's just say that usually, I shower after this, letting the water awaken me a bit more, and I dress into the clothes that only Brittney would wear, something floral paired with something neutral, entirely unique to any other outfit on campus, a bring scrunchie slipped onto one wrist, a chakra stone in my pocket. My mornings are relatively quiet and peaceful, for I must be considerate to my roommate, and I'm *always* running late to class.

I step outside my dorm hall and somehow, it is both sunny and thunder storming all at once. The air is humid and hot and lingers on the back of my neck. I power walk to class and stare at all of the people, some of which I've met before and some of who I've never seen. I look at the swaying trees and admire how the birds glide between them, and I glance at the construction and try to make some sort of beauty out of it, give it some sort of story. Sometimes my headphones are in and I'm blaring 60's or 80's, anything to freshen my head, and sometimes I only listen to the sound of the busy, yet calming morning, eavesdropping on the drowsy chatter and hearing the sound of bicycle tires racing against the pavement.

In class, I listen. Mostly. Sometimes I blink and class is over and I have forgotten to write anything down. Sometimes I raise my hand and answer every question. Sometimes I make jokes under my breath just to steal snickers from classmates. Sometimes I say nothing and smile with my lips pressed tight together. It really depends on how strong the coffee was.

I grab coffee (yes, *more* coffee) with my sweet boyfriend and go to class again and normally, I just draw out my dreams in my bullet journal, planning out my future, or just planning out my dinner plans. I'm always so desperate about dinner plans.

Class is over and it is time for work. I have a desk job that is located in a drabby, gray building, so I decorate my desk with coffee mugs and pretty scrapbook paper and photographs of my simple little life. Sometimes my coworkers are there, and we all chat about our classes and general lives, but it can be challenging to participate in conversation because I am only a freshman and they are seniors and have extravagant lives that I haven't had the pleasure of grazing just yet. I'm almost there, anyways.

Sometimes, I am alone, and I plug in my headphones and knock out my assignments while sipping on some dandelion tea--the dining hall food doesn't always sit well, to say the least.

Work is over. I walk back to my dorm and it takes nearly twenty minutes because I walk slowly, absorbing everything I see. Either I grab some dinner with friends and we hang out afterwards or I exercise at the gym with a friend or I am out with my family or I am staying in with my boyfriend or I am with *someone*, at least. Rarely am I alone--I make sure of it, even if being alone is what I need.

At rare times, I *am* alone, and after a little while of struggling, I sink deep down into the comforting silence that is darkness accompanied by a few lit candles.

At night, I am with my roommate and we talk about our days and then we reside to our own spaces, which are only a few feet apart. I work on homework, do some studying, and then I read a little or watch a movie before bed.

Now, there *was* a point to this. I didn't just write about my average college day and expect that to help anyone in any spectacular way, at least.

Before I go to sleep, I think about this day. I think about the people I interacted with and I wonder if I showed enough emotion while speaking to them. I wonder if I showed enough of myself. I wonder if I did enough to benefit who I am tomorrow. I wonder if I am in the right place with the right people in the right major doing the right things and then I wonder and wonder and I can't stop wondering. I stare at the ceiling in amazement at how my life has changed so drastically, how I was once a sweet high schooler who wrote books and now, I am an independent woman who hardly writes at all but misses it dearly and is slowly finding her way in this giant college world.

Sometimes, when I look at myself in the mirror, look at what I'm wearing, look at how I smile, I don't recognize myself. This girl that I am has changed. I interact with so many different people, it's often easy to lose myself among the crowd. These days… they blur by, blending together into one large watercolor painting. These emotions I feel... I feel them so strongly, and I forget where they come from and when they first appeared. Half of my mind is crowded with who I once was and the other half is crowded with who I could be and a small sliver in the middle is everything that I *am*. It's difficult to see, but it's there. My thoughts are constantly battling with one another as they lead me in one direction and then another and then backwards and I realize in this moment that I need to take control of the words that flutter inside and convince me that I am smaller than I am.

I fall asleep somewhere within my thoughts and I wake up early the next day and decide to meditate, journal a bit, so I do, and then after I do I walk over to the mirror and peer at myself. I can see myself a little more clearly today, and I smile at my reflection. It is early and yet, my thoughts are already racing. I try to silence them by inhaling... exhaling.... It works, just a little. Then, I smile a bit brighter, because this is a new day, a new me, and I am here, *now*.

In just a few months, even less, my life will change again. My life is always changing, flourishing into something new, so I might as well take everything as it is while I am here, whether it is a battle to find myself, or not. Surely, I am in the right place--it's as right as it can be, because I found my way here, didn't I? This life, everything that makes it up, was built upon my own choices made within my own mind. And I couldn't be more proud of where I progressed to. To some, I may be just another freshman classmate, just another friendly face, but within, I am so much more.

This is our life. Right now. This is what it is--this is what you get. You might miss home sometimes and you might regret a few things and you might fear what the future holds and you might be carrying quite a lot on your shoulders and you might be struggling to find yourself and you may compare yourself often, but at some point you must realize that these thoughts don't actually exist and you are in control of everything you are.

Anyways, I hope you enjoyed your stay within this chaotic, magical place that is my mind. Until next time!

Brittney Kristina is the author of *Forsaken* and *Fifty Days*, both of which she published as a teenager. When she's not writing, she's nose-deep in a book, sipping from a large mug of coffee or tea, outside in nature, or gushing over psychological theories.

Follow her on Instagram @Brittney.Kristina or find her at www.brittneykristina.com.

Made in the USA
Monee, IL
24 September 2021